Killer Whale Blues

Killer Whale Blues

A Novel

Mark Conkling

SUNSTONE
PRESS

SANTA FE

Sunstone books may be purchased for educational, business, or sales promotional use.
For information please write: Special Markets Department, Sunstone Press,
P.O. Box 2321, Santa Fe, New Mexico 87504-2321.

Book and Cover design › Vicki Ahl
Body typeface › Constantia
Printed on acid-free paper
∞
eBook 978-1-61139-224-1

Library of Congress Cataloging-in-Publication Data

Conkling, Mark, 1941-
    Killer whale blues : a novel / by Mark Conkling.
        pages cm
    ISBN 978-0-86534-981-0 (softcover : alk. paper)
    1. Killer whale--Fiction. 2. Redemption--Fiction. 3. Human-animal relationships-
-Fiction. I. Title.
    PS3603.O535K55 2013
    813'.6--dc23

                                2013043436

WWW.SUNSTONEPRESS.COM
SUNSTONE PRESS / POST OFFICE BOX 2321 / SANTA FE, NM 87504-2321 /USA
(505) 988-4418 / ORDERS ONLY (800) 243-5644 / FAX (505) 988-1025

Killer Whale Blues
is dedicated to my sons
Bryan and Daniel

Acknowledgements

I am grateful to my writing friends and others who have taken valuable time to read my work and to offer helpful comments: Jonis Agee, Robert Boswell, Nancy Best, Nancy Dickeman, Barbara Corn Patterson, Michelle Sauceda-Halliday, José Toledo, Dwight Hilson, Kristen-Paige Madona, Rochelle Williams, Vicky Chavez, and Kim Hamel. The world brightens when I come out of my own mind.

*A*nd so we came forth,
and once again beheld the stars.

—William Styron

1

Every so often unexpected things happen, sudden changes from which you can't come back, even if you want to, because once you get started, the path rolls up behind you, snapping at your heels, driving you forward with sharp little nips at the back of your soul. Some say it was fate that made strange things happen to Ida May Corley—a troubled woman of 36, an intensive care nurse with soft curves, dusty blond hair, puffy lips, and an empty heart—while others say she brought these strange things on herself as she tried to claw her way out of her misery.

Ida lived in Albuquerque with her lover Danny, thought about getting married, feared getting pregnant, couldn't sleep, and for the last month, her best friend at work told her a dozen times she looked like crap—completely burned out. "You drag yourself into the nurses' station, you snap and snarl at everyone, and by midnight you're unbearable. You can't keep this up, Ida—you're coming unglued."

Ida chewed on a thumbnail. "It's been over a year, Marge, and I still smell her perfume in the house—you can't imagine the burden I have. All of Mother's stuff is still there. My father and brothers won't move anything. They're helpless. I have to work to forget."

"That's the problem—you're blind to yourself. Medical people can't see their own burnout. They just keep going. Work harder, do more. I swear you're going to have a stroke or something. Look at your hands—they're shaking."

Ida looked and crossed her arms.

"I've seen you take uppers in the night. Are you taking sleeping pills when you get home?"

Ida frowned and looked to the left at a beeping monitor, raised her hand and began twisting her hair. "I'm just tired. This past year took its toll.

I love Danny, but I'm tired from all the shit he put me through. It was a good cause, but I'm afraid we'll never be the same."

"Come on, Ida. You stood by him, you attended him in the hospital, you supported him—you were in the shit because you chose to be."

Ida paced back and forth, arms crossed. "Sometimes he really pisses me off."

Marge grabbed her wrist and pulled Ida's face close. "What about this long-sleeve jersey under your scrubs? I know you've picked your arms raw. Keep this up and I'll have to haul you off to the loony bin. Are you scheduled for a long weekend over Thanksgiving?"

"No, I'm working."

"You're stubborn as they come. I'm telling you, Ida, you're going to lose it."

Ida pulled loose. "I'm going down to the cafeteria for a break. I need to think." She hurried onto the elevator, went in the cafeteria, grabbed some coffee and chose a table in a dark corner. The coffee tasted like acid in her throat.

Stubborn? Probably. Burned out? *I don't think so.* She had resisted going through her dead mother's things, especially her handmade quilts, and her weird collection of dozens of new, unworn panties. What was that about? Neatly packed away in white tissue paper were regular pink, blue, and white silk panties; red, maroon, and beige hipsters with tiny matching bows on the sides; skinny, high-rise bikinis, pastel wisps of flimsy fabric; and lacy green, mauve, and mocha thongs from Victoria's Secret. Over the years, her mother, Janice Corley, had bought all sizes, from small, for the shapely hips she had as a young woman, to the full-size cotton briefs she wore before she succumbed to diapers and to her soft, flannel hospital dress—a light blue and white death gown, the very one Ida's father brought home from the funeral home and hung in the closet, unwashed, still carrying her smell. During that time, her hospice bed was framed by the window that looked out to Albuquerque's Sandia Mountains, her favorite view. Frail and cancer-ridden, surrounded by vases of fresh flowers, she spent her last days with her family and a hospice nurse. Greeting cards addressed to "Mom" covered her nightstand, the only name most people knew. Mom died peacefully there, on the 15-acre homestead off Eubank, next to the Corley Prairie Dog Park, the family business. Ida and Mom had never gotten along well, although they had cooked holiday meals together, rather, Ida had helped Mom with cooking, and they shared a sometime hobby of collecting first edition books. Although often annoyed with Mom's choices, Ida enjoyed the outings, the escape from work, and the alluring search through dusty bookstore shelves. Mom was proud of her first editions of Martin Buber's *I and Thou*, Paul Tillich's *The Courage to Be*, and Lee Strobel's *The Case for Christ*; Ida favored her Hemmingway, *The Sun Also Rises*, Steinbeck's *Of Mice and Men,* and Sylvia Plath's *The Bell Jar*. Over the years, their collections came to occupy separate shelves on opposite sides of the living room—their erstwhile hobby fading along with Mom's illness. That was the extent of any meaningful relationship between them except for what happened on that one special day. It was a sad day, 19 months ago, just after July 4, 2002. Ida's eyes watered as she remembered the conversation that wove them together in a family secret and into a cherished, intimate trust.

Ida had changed Mom's colostomy bag, washed her face, brushed her hair, and helped her slip on a fresh gown.

Mom took a sip of water. "I think I could eat some yogurt."

Ida got a small cup from the refrigerator and helped Mom take a couple of bites.

"Do you need another patch?" Ida asked.

"No, I'm fine. I don't want to sleep so much."

"Sleeping is normal. Your body needs it."

"Do you really like your new boyfriend Danny?"

Ida raised her eyebrows, turning her head. "I've surprised myself. I like him a lot. He doesn't have any money, and he's not flashy, but there's something very genuine about him. He loves animals and has a way with dogs."

"Is he good in bed?"

Ida smiled. "Mother, what kind of question is that?"

"Good sex is important. Most relationships don't last without it. Well, is he?"

"He's gentle and a very good lover."

"That's good. You ought to marry him. You know he's a good sponsor for Junior. Danny has supported him since he got out of rehab. I think he would be good for you."

"Remember, Mom? That's when I met Danny, there in the family visiting room."

"Oh, I didn't remember. Those days were such a blur. You should marry him, Ida."

"Well, he has to ask me, don't you think?"

"Come on, you know very well how to steer a man—that shouldn't be too hard. After all, you're quite a catch."

"You've never talked like this. What in the world has gotten into you?"

"I don't want you to waste time. Your biological clock will kick in soon. I wish I could live to see your children."

"I don't want kids yet. I want to get my master's degree first—that's a couple of years."

Mom reached for Ida's hand and pulled her close. "I want to tell you something. I think it's time. I know you can keep a secret."

Ida leaned closer and Mom whispered in her ear. "When I was seventeen, before I met your father, I had an abortion."

Ida pulled away, taking a deep breath. "Oh, I didn't know. Did Grandmother Hawthorn know?"

"Yes, Mother knew. We took a trip to Canada, stayed with her friend, and I had it done in Victoria. After we came home, we never spoke of it again. I sometimes wonder how my life might have turned out if I'd had the baby."

Ida put her hand on Mom's shoulder. "I never imagined."

"I want you to find the right man and get married so you won't ever have to go through that. It's too painful. It still haunts me."

Ida raised Mom's weak hand up to her face and kissed it. Then Ida put her head down on the pillow next to Mom's face. "We'll be okay, we'll be okay." Mom's tears dripped into the space between their hands, as if to create a seal of generational pain, an eternal and trusted secret between mother and daughter, their last private conversation before Mom died.

Sort through her stuff? Clean out her closet? Empty her hope chest?— Jesus, her father wouldn't shut up about the hope chest. Ida had seen inside the chest only once, another peculiar time back then after everyone learned that Mom was fatally ill.. She could still picture the morning because it was so weird. After the hospice nurse left, Mom had led Ida to her walk-in closet, opened the large hope chest with a key, and showed her each of the nine handmade quilts, tenderly tracing the stitches and patterns as she recalled stories of when she made them. Then, as if performing a teenage show-and-tell, Mom stood and smiled, held up two pair of new panties, twirled around on one foot, waved them in the air, and then put them away. "They're so much fun to buy, don't you think?"

Ida helped Mom sit down as she coughed and caught her breath, kneeling in front of her. Ida tipped her head and raised her eyebrows. "When did you buy all these?"

"Over the years. I watch for sales, you know."

"You've never worn them. Are, ah...were you saving them for something?"

"No, not any more," she sighed. "They're nothing but old dreams."

Ida gazed out the window, crossing her arms. "What should I do with these things?"

"Please give one quilt to each of the women in my prayer group, and keep your favorite one for your bed. Take some of the panties to feel pretty, and give the rest to a thrift store. Please don't let your father see them." Mom refolded them carefully. Each pair had a little white label with a date written in black ink.

Later that night, Ida wondered if the panties helped Mom imagine the woman she might have been, perhaps a fantasy parade through her imagination, secret thrills from the past, but why was each pair labeled? Why in the world would she date them by month, day, and year?

Cafeteria dishes clattered as someone dropped a tray. Ida wiped her eyes with a tissue and blew her nose. She jumped up from the cafeteria table, ran to the women's bathroom, splashed water on her face, looked in the mirror, and turned away from the image of her gray ashen face. Burned out? Unglued? She popped a little white pill in her mouth, drank water from her hand, smoothed her hair, and scooted to the ICU. No burnout here. She had a room full of critical patients waiting.

A year and a half had passed, and on the second Christmas after Mom's death, Roy Corley, who everyone called Pop, helped Ida clear the big table and followed her into the kitchen. They tossed the empty Kentucky Fried Chicken buckets and leftover coleslaw into a large black plastic garbage can inside the back door. Ida shook her head. Dirty oatmeal bowls, dried out hot dog buns, and an open carton of milk littered the countertop, and the stainless steel sink was water stained and full of crusty dishes. Mom was probably rolling over in her grave. She had prepared a full-course dinner every Christmas, and kept a spotless kitchen.

Pop turned and looked at her. "Ida, I've been meaning to ask you something."

She crossed her arms and glared. "I don't want to talk about Mom."

"I know, but whenever I try to work out in the machine shop, your mom's private things make me sad. I hate to keep asking, but could you at least go through that big chest and get rid of the quilts and things?"

Ida's green eyes flashed, and she raised both hands and tightened her blond ponytail. "What about Jeff or Junior? Can't they help? Put the stuff in storage somewhere."

Pop reached in his pocket and handed Ida a small key. "Mom said she wanted you to do it—you'd know what to keep and what to give away. She insisted."

Ida turned her back. "I can't do it today."

"Here, at least take the key. Maybe you can get to it later this week."

Ida grabbed the key and pushed it into the back pocket of her jeans. "Next week I work clear through New Year's Day. Maybe I can come by Friday morning, after you and Junior go to work."

"Thanks. Mom's death is hard for me too." Tentatively, he reached his hand toward her, but she ignored it and dried her hands.

"I'm not promising."

"Okay." His wizened face took on the hint of a smile as he looked down. "Merry Christmas."

"Merry Christmas, Pop, but I've got to go. I told Danny I'd be home so we could have Christmas dinner, too."

Ida drove out past the gate, down Corley Lane, and onto Eubank, Paseo to I-25, and then to the south valley acreage where she and Danny lived with his dog, a black terrier cross named Jedi, and her little tan Pug named ER. Jedi was a rescue dog. Danny's veterinarian friend had brought Jedi to him soon after his dog named Lucky had been killed by a car. ER was Ida's little full-bred Pug she had rescued from the shelter in Santa Fe soon after Mom had died. Danny and Jedi had recently become a dog-therapy team, and they worked two days a week at Presbyterian Hospital, and one day at the University Hospital. As a self-styled dog whisperer, Danny also taught dog training at the Pet Smart stores on the weekends, and with her work as a certified intensive care nurse, they made a good living.

Last year had been incredibly dramatic and life changing—Danny was hurt in a van fire saving rescue dogs, and she was almost fired through the efforts of a nasty lawyer. It all started when Danny was laid off from his job as a Vet Tech at the animal shelter for what some people called his big mouth, but others called his passionate sense of justice. He had accused the owner of a private no-kill animal rescue center of running a scam, mistreating animals, and diverting charitable donations. The owner had come after Danny with a tough lawyer and outright vengeance, and Ida, through no fault of her own except loving Danny, got embroiled in the whole mess and arose to his defense. Danny's burns were healing well, and Ida was looking forward to a quiet, normal existence, a time where she and Danny could settle in and maybe even get married. She admired his sense of justice and his connection to animals. He believed that he could communicate across species, and he often talked with his dogs with both words and touch. Any dog who approached Danny sniffed once or twice, and then settled, as though Danny and dogs shared the same world. He had given up a year of his life and almost lost his five years of sobriety in the legal battle—a battle that ended with good outcomes for the dogs, but pushed Danny into the winds of misfortune. A major donor for the no-kill shelter moved away, the shady owner gave up the no-kill shelter, and Danny suffered in the horrible fire in an animal rescue van. The fire happened in a shopping center parking lot, and Danny had rushed into the burning van and pulled all the dogs out, saving their lives. The burns on his hands and face put him in the hospital for a month, and during his healing, as if driven by fate, he wandered through a new door in his life. Ida brought Jedi to the hospital, and soon after, Danny and Jedi visited dozens of patients on the cancer ward, clearly, Danny believed, some kind of calling. Just weeks later, and after some training, they became a therapy-dog team, a source of pain relief and laughter for many hospitalized patients. Danny was a good man, a little wacky now and then, but decent and morally upstanding. Ida could imagine them building a sturdy life together, and she desperately wanted some peace of mind, a mental state that persistently outran her, always a few steps ahead, just out of reach.

The very thought of having to go through her mother's stuff made a dull pain behind her heart. She chewed her bottom lip as she pulled into the driveway. Danny was standing at the door, eyes bright with a smile, hands on his hips, and a white apron down to his knees over his khaki shorts, making him look like he had no pants on. Ida laughed as she got out of the car, walked up to him, her puffy pink lips open and inviting a kiss. Then she relaxed into his arms, her full breasts against his chest, and her face pressed to his ear. "I'm glad to be home with you. I don't like going out to the old house." The dull pain persisted.

Danny took her hands, pushed her back, and caught her eyes with his. "Hey, I know it's tough. I miss Mom, too. Let's go in, it's cold. I made pasta."

"I told Pop I might go through her big trunk—next week."

"Want me to go?"

"I'm not sure I'm going. If I do, it's better if I'm by myself, when everyone's gone."

On Friday morning, the day after April Fool's Day, Ida paused, fascinated by a new purple crocus by the porch, the first sign of spring. She went back in the house, put on her old jeans and a sweatshirt, and tied her soft blond hair in a ponytail with a green ribbon. She kissed Danny quickly, handed him the grocery list, and turned to the door. "You go to the store, okay? I'm going out to the house. I can't put it off any longer. Pop called again. At least I need to go through her hope chest."

Danny ran his hand through his tousled dark hair. "Want any help?"

"No, I have to do this alone."

Ida drove quickly across town, stopping at a Starbucks for a latte, then at a Walgreens for Tylenol. She couldn't shake a persistent dizzy feeling; there was pressure on her chest, and she was bloated from persistent constipation. Though her thoughts raced, she simply could not gather them into a coherent idea except for one. She was angry. She knew that. Angry at her boss, angry at her ICU patients, angry at her brothers, and sometimes, for no reason she understood, she wanted to slap Danny or whoever was nearby. Three weeks ago, on purpose, she jerked out a man's catheter too quickly. For days, she felt guilty about his screams. She parked behind the house and let herself in the dark machine shop that smelled of oil and sawdust, filled with memories of her father repairing equipment, and sitting on his lap at his old desk. The smell of burnt, perked coffee on the wood stove seemed to linger beside his stack of dusty parts catalogs. When she was little, they had laughed together as he showed her pictures of loaders, bulldozers, backhoes, motor graders, and ditch diggers. Often she sat in his lap as he moved equipment around the yard. Sometimes he let her raise the bucket on the loader and dump dirt into a pile.

She pulled the string on an overhead light, closed the door, wheeled Pop's old office chair over by the chest, and opened Mom's musty hope chest with the key. The folded quilts lay neatly on top and completely covered the piles of panties, still labeled neatly with their dates. A sealed envelope addressed to Ida lay under the first pair.

Dear Ida,

There are many ways to deal with temptation. This was my way, and maybe you will find it useful. Whenever I felt lust for another man, I would buy a pair of panties, label them with the date, and put them away. Then I would pray that the feelings would leave by the end of that day, and they usually did. It helped to know that date was dead and gone. I never did understand why this worked, but I think it was mostly the prayers. Love, Mom.

Ida gritted her teeth and shook her head. Her mother tempted by lust for other men? There was over *thirty* pair of panties. Jesus, Mom. *What went on in your mind?* Ida stood, tore the letter into little pieces, put them in the stove, and pushed them under the ashes with a poker. She sat back down, took a deep breath, and gently peeled the date labels off each pair, wrapping them back in their tissue paper. The dates were about one year apart, always in the winter.

Underneath, on the bottom, she found a leather-bound Bible, sat down, and began paging through the worn pages, looking at marked passages on the pages with dog-eared corners. These were words her mother had believed, words she had enshrined on plaques around the house: *do unto others as you would do unto yourself; judge not lest ye be judged; love one another as I have loved you; love the Lord your God with all your heart.*

She put the Bible on her lap, folded her hands, let her head fall back against the chair. Tears flowed as she thought about the last weeks of Mom's life. In those final days, they had held hands, shared intimate moments alone, and Mom had confessed her secret abortion. Now that moment was written on the petals of the pink roses that blossomed over Mom's ashes, the place just outside the window where she was laid to rest. After 20 years of Mom's insistent worry and judgment, Ida's deception and secret life with men, and their inability to ever look into one another's eyes, they finally had achieved peace and harmony between them.

She wiped her tears with the sleeve of her sweatshirt, blew her nose into a tissue, and leafed again through the Bible. Pages in the middle of the *Song of Solomon* were slightly separated. *What's this?* She turned the Bible over and shook it. A slim, yellowed tissue envelope fell out. She opened it carefully, and pulled out a faded letter written in pencil on Big Chief ruled notebook paper with wide lines.

Dear Janice,

I'm glad you are back. A boy. That's great! I'm glad he's safe with good parents. I told people you were at a special summer school in Vancouver. I'm really sorry your mother won't let me see you any more. She told me to stay away, but I will always be near you. I will love you forever. XOXO, Fred.

Ida took a deep breath, carefully put the letter back in the Bible, tucked the Bible back in the chest under the quilts, dropped to her knees on the floor, put her shaking hands over her face, and began to rock back and forth for a long time. When she noticed her knees hurting, Ida pulled up her sweatshirt and wiped her face, biting her lip. She unfolded and then folded all the quilts but one, put them in a plastic bag, and marked the bag "For Janice Corley's Prayer Group" with a black marker. Except for a few hipsters and one pink thong that Danny would like, she put all the panties in another bag and marked it "For the Thrift Store." She made her way to the car as though her legs were wooden, threw the bags in the back, opened the front door, slipped in, gripped the steering wheel with white fingers and knuckles, and drove fast to the Sandia Tram parking lot. She screeched to a stop in a shady spot, took a breath, and shook her head, hoping to find a way to piece things together. Her armpits dripped sweat as she read the letter again, and then screamed at the windshield until her face was purple.

That magical moment—the frail time of deep trust with Mom on her deathbed—drifted out the open window and floated away like wispy gray smoke disappearing into the blue sky. From the center of Ida's mind, a strong irritation arose and, without hesitation, began fighting for a place, pushing itself into the tangle of other irritations already living there, all jostling for position like sharp-elbowed women at a Walmart holiday sale. Over the years, Ida had fashioned a walled-in space in her mind where she packed her fear and anger, a wonky, protected space wrapped by the warmth of men, their dependable and unending desires for her body, and her bustling control of her work and those around her. She was often haunted by the fear she could not handle everything, and that her life would one day fly apart in little pieces, like silver glitter in the wind.

Her head hummed inside like a tuning fork. Mom had lied to her about the abortion. She had a baby, and had given her son away to a couple in Canada. Jesus, she just gave him away. Ida gripped the steering wheel, lips quivering, and rocked as she counted. Mom was seventeen the year she went to Canada in 1959 and had her baby. Somewhere, if he was alive, there was a half brother who was 44, eight years older than she was. Her mother was a freaking liar and Ida had a half brother—damn. Mom insisted that she be the one who went through the chest. Mom knew that she'd find the letter, and that she'd shield Pop from knowing Mom had a son by a different man. Ida had been used, jammed up between Mom and Pop to hide the truth. *And who the hell is Fred?*

The next Tuesday, as Ida dropped off her tax return at the post office, her cell phone buzzed. It was her brother Jeff. "Hi, can you do me a favor? I need a ride to work tomorrow."

"Car problems?"

"No, I've got to drop my car off for service. They said it would take all day. It's the Lexus dealer on San Mateo."

"I'm working the night shift, so I could come by the dealer about eight."

"That would be great."

Jeff was waiting outside when Ida drove up. "Do you have a full day of patients?"

"A couple of crowns and one implant, but my first appointment isn't until ten. Ida, are you all right? You look stressed."

Ida pulled a twist of hair between her lips, and drove to Jeff's office in silence. "Hey, why don't you come in? I'll make some coffee."

They went into Jeff's office and he poured two cups. "What's going on? You don't seem yourself."

Ida paced, breathing hard. "Do you know much about Mom's teen-age life?"

"She never said much. I remember her saying Grandmother Hawthorn kept her on a short leash, especially after Grandpa Russ died. That was when she was about twelve."

"That's what I remember." Ida stood up, walked into the hall, and stopped at Mom's smiling photo featured on the wall. She slapped the frame, knocking the picture off the wall. "She's a bitch."

Jeff picked up the photo, tapping the shards of glass into a wastebasket. "What the hell's the matter with you? Those crowns are some of my best work...a twenty-five-thousand-dollar smile."

Ida turned and raced into the bathroom. She fell onto her knees by the toilet, grabbed the seat with both hands, and vomited until her throat and stomach felt like fire. After washing her face, she found Jeff in his office. He tipped his head sideways. "I'm worried—are you sick?"

"I cleaned out Mom's hope chest."

"Pop worries himself sick about her stuff."

"I found an old letter."

"A letter?"

"A letter from a guy named Fred, when Mom was about seventeen. Ever heard of Fred?"

"A love letter?"

"More than that. Mom told me on her deathbed that she had an abortion when she was seventeen."

Jeff raised his eyebrows. "Wow, I never knew."

"So guess what. She lied to me. The letter said she had a baby boy, born in Canada, about six years before you were born."

Jeff looked up at the ceiling and took a deep breath. "Grandmother Hawthorn had some dear friends in Canada—I think near Vancouver. Do you think Mom could have...?"

"She had a boyfriend named Fred. Her mother took her to Canada. She had a baby boy." Ida dug in her jacket pocket and handed the letter to Jeff.

He read it twice. "You can't say anything about this. It'll put Pop in an early grave."

"She lied to me. There was no abortion. We have a half brother!"

"That was forty-some years ago. He may not even be alive."

"If he is we have a sibling."

"There's nothing to be gained by dredging it up. Just let it be." He handed her the letter.

"Burn this."

Jeff reached into the bottom drawer of his desk and took out a cigar box. "And while you're at it, go through this stuff and make sure there's nothing incriminating."

"What's this?"

"Pop gave me this box and said to save whatever I wanted. It was in Mom's dresser."

Ida opened the box and began sorting through decals, souvenirs, and a few old photos. There were yellowed decals and matchbooks from Carlsbad Caverns, Disneyland, SeaWorld, and the Grand Canyon. Three old, labeled, crumpled envelopes contained locks of hair—Junior, Ida, and Jeff. There were several old black-and-white photos of Junior, Ida, Jeff, and Mom and Pop. They were labeled with Mom's handwriting on the back,

"Disneyworld 1972, Carlsbad Caverns, 1974." There was a picture of Jeff and Junior with Goofy, and one of Ida with Minnie Mouse.

Ida shuffled the photos. "These are when I was four and six."

"Yeah, I remember that picture with Goofy. Pop took it. He said he would get all three Goofy guys in the same picture."

Ida picked out a motel key with a green tag that said, "Thunderbird Motel, Route 66, #22."

"Shit, do you know anything about this?"

"Nope. That motel was down on Central Avenue. It's gone now."

"Maybe that was Mom and Fred's love nest."

Jeff stood up and put his hands on his hips. "Let it go, Ida—the past is gone. If you say anything to Pop, I'll call you a liar."

Ida pushed the key in her pocket. She held up a cork coaster. "What about this?"

Jeff took it. "There's a drawing of a building—says Empress Hotel, Victoria. This is really old."

Ida took an envelope from Jeff's desk. She placed the coaster carefully inside, folded the envelope, and put it in her pocket.

"You should throw everything out. Don't make a mess, Ida. We've had enough problems."

Ida stood up and walked to the door. "You keep the rest of the stuff. I don't need the memories."

Jeff touched her shoulder. "I'm telling you. Let this be. If Pop finds out he'll have a heart attack. I'll call Junior. He needs to know."

"Meet me at Chili's for dinner? We can talk through it—see if we remember anything else."

"You've got to promise we'll keep this whole thing quiet."

After work, Jeff drove to the Corley place and parked by the barn. It was getting dark and both Pop and Junior were fussing and drinking coffee. "Hey, what are you guys working on?" Jeff asked.

Pop switched off a small vibrating sander and looked up. "What brings you here? Did you leave work early?"

"My last patient cancelled—a couple of nice crowns—but at least she rescheduled."

"You work too much anyway," Junior said.

Jeff shook his head. "You're right. This solo practice gets to be a drag."

Pop poured Jeff a mug of coffee and handed it to him. "Sit down. Take a load off."

"How did things go at the park today?" Jeff asked.

"Sold over two hundred tickets—a good day. Pop got the trails watered. We had two busloads from schools. Those little kids love to chatter at the prairie dogs."

"Who would have ever thought? The Corley family makes a living from a prairie dog park. Mom was sure proud of us. I miss her."

Pop took off his cap, smoothed his hair, and put the cap back on.

Junior stood up and looked out the window. "Sometimes her absence seems bigger than her presence."

"We need to get over it," Pop said.

Jeff motioned to the bench. "What are you making?"

"A cedar chest for Ida. I thought it would be a good wedding present."

The chest was small, about 16" by 24", with a rounded lid, copper hinges, and copper straps on the front, top, and back.

"How long have you been working on this?"

Pop grinned, ear-to-ear. "A long time. I knew Ida would get married one day."

"It looks like a treasure chest," Jeff said. "She'll love it."

Pop opened the lid. Jeff looked inside and smelled the rich odor of cedar. The wood fit together perfectly.

"I can't get over being sad," Junior said, "but it's getting a little easier."

"The wedding's still in August, right?" Pop asked.

Jeff turned toward the door. "Danny said they're shooting for Saturday, August seventh. They're happy about having it here at the house."

"I want it out behind the house," Pop said, "where we buried Mom's ashes. It's a good place."

"Got to go," Jeff said. "I'm meeting our accountant."

Pop touched the top of the cedar chest, his finger tracing one of the copper straps. "Don't say anything about the cedar chest. It's a surprise."

Jeff sat outside Chili's. Junior walked up and Danny was with him. They had just come from a six pm AA meeting. They settled into a large corner booth. Junior turned to Jeff.

"What's going on? It sounded important."

Jeff glanced at Danny.

"It's okay. Danny knows everything. We don't have any secrets."

"Ida will be here soon. She found an old letter. It seems we have a half brother. Mom had a baby when she was seventeen. Ida thinks she gave him away to someone in Canada, maybe to some friends of Grandmother Hawthorn."

Junior shook his head. "Are you sure? Our mother?"

Just then Ida appeared, sat down between Danny and Junior, and took the letter from her jacket pocket. She opened it and flattened the page out on the table. "Read this." They both read it. Junior put one hand over his mouth. "Jeeze, this is incredible. We've got a half brother somewhere."

Danny raised his eyebrows. "Everything changes when something changes."

Jeff leaned in. "No, it doesn't have to. We need to keep this quiet."

Junior looked at Danny. "You know Pop and his blood pressure. Jeff's right. This news would do him in."

Ida folded the letter carefully. "I can't stand it. I have to know."

"Mom probably thought it was better this way," Junior said, touching Ida's arm. "She loved us all, you know."

"You don't understand. Mom and I never connected until just before she died. I finally had some peace around that. But it turned out it was all a lie. Don't you see? Now it's worse." Ida rubbed her face with both hands. "It's all jumbled up. If she was alive, I feel like I'd kill her."

Junior nodded. "I was that angry. Danny remembers, right?"

Danny smiled through blue eyes immersed in dark worry and put one hand on Ida's back. They ordered salads and sandwiches and ate in silence, Ida sniffling, Danny softly rubbing her back. Ida picked at the food, tossed her fork on the table, and put her hand on her chin, facing the wall.

Jeff put his fork down. "Here's the deal. We swear right now no one will tell Pop. I'm going to forget about it, and, Junior, you should too. Burn the letter, Ida. This didn't happen. Got it?"

Ida looked up at Jeff and Junior. "I can live with that for now."

The rest of April and most of May brought a rash of new problems into Ida's life. Angry images disturbed her sleep, grimacing faces of strange men, and recurrent dreams of people in hospital gowns pouring out buckets of dirty mop water under her feet. In order to chase them off, she had to slosh through the filthy water, shooing them off with a wet broom. When she awoke, nausea gripped her for hours.

Each night at work, it took more effort to smile at patients and to listen to family members. She couldn't sit still, and for a couple of weeks she had felt bloated and fat. She had missed one period, but was waiting for her next one before she picked up a pregnancy test from the drugstore. Late one night at work, she doubled over with cramps and began bleeding heavily. In the bathroom, she looked carefully at her discharge. Was it a miscarriage?

Two weeks later at work, fighting back a shadowy sense of darkness, an old boyfriend, an anesthetist at the hospital, came up behind Ida. He gently touched her shoulder and smiled. "Let's go for a walk."

"Oh, Doug, how have you been? This is awkward. You know I'm engaged now. Is there something you want to talk about?" Her face flushed. Desire radiated from him, making hot, wavy shadows in the air. He smiled, and she was drawn to his warmth. His breath smelled like cinnamon. "Have you seen the new wing? Let's take a break."

Ida walked along beside him as he led her to the elevator, up two floors, and through a corridor that led to a closed ward. "They're going to open this wing in a couple of days. Check it out."

They walked down the silent hallway lit only by nightlights. He stopped, opened a door, and led Ida into a room with a sparkling new tile floor, walls with fresh light green paint, and two beds with new pillows and sheets—a white curtain drawn partway between them. The air smelled sweet, like orange floor cleaner, and cold, blue, mercury-vapor lights shined in from the parking lot. He put his hands on Ida's shoulders and turned her toward him. "You seem like you need a friend. Are things okay at home? Tell me what's going on."

Ida looked down, thinking about the weekends she used to have with Doug, the times he took her to Las Vegas, the all-nighters at the craps table, the champagne, her smell of early morning sex, his Mickey Mouse tattoo over his naval, and the luxurious sleep until late afternoon. "Everything is fine. I'm just tired. I haven't been sleeping well." She let Doug lift her face in his hands. He kissed her gently, touching her lips with his tongue, like before. She turned her face, a warm shiver rippling up her back, her knees nearly buckling. "This is not good. We should go back now."

"Not good? You've got to be kidding. We've always been great together. Remember?"

Ida smiled at him. "Yes, I remember. And now you're going to tell me what I need, right?" She loved being desired by good-smelling men—a sumptuous feeling, much like feathers on her skin and floating on soft pillows, a place far away from her confusion and irritation. Someday those men will get you in serious trouble, her mother had warned, and you'll end up getting an abortion.

"How about what we both need? We're good together, and you're still the most beautiful woman I've ever known."

Ida shook her head, put her arms around him as he pulled her close, kissing her neck, and began swaying in a rocking dance step, his Mickey Mouse tattoo rubbing softly under her breasts, until the starchy sheets on the bed touched the back of her legs. She leaned forward and pushed her hands against his chest. "This is not going to happen."

"What's going on? You love what I do."

"Not now I don't." She pushed past him, rushed out the door, and scurried to the elevator. She flashed a pasty smile over her shoulder as she got off the elevator ahead of him. "Back to work," she said. "Nice to see you again." His frown disappeared behind the elevator doors.

Ida spent most nights at work with her stomach clenched and teeth gritted. She had been promoted to charge nurse for the night shift in the ICU, a sterile place she could control, yet each night she lost some of her focus and shuffled through clouds of despair. In mid-May, she made some serious mistakes with injections—one night she gave the wrong medication to one of her patients, and it caused a bad reaction. She came home the next morning with a gray face and dull eyes. "I've got to do something about this."

Danny sat down beside her. "I'm sorry. Can I help?"

"I'm going. I'm going to search for him."

"I worry about you just taking off, especially by yourself. Maybe he doesn't want to be found, have you thought about that?"

"I'll figure that out later. There's part of my life that's missing—it haunts me."

"Where will you go?"

"Well, I found a clue. I have a name and a city."

"A name?"

"I went through the sign-in book for Mom's funeral. I recognized most of the people, but there was one strange name. A man signed in as 'Joel Martin, Victoria, Vancouver Island, Canada, old friend.' Why would a man from Canada be at Mom's funeral? A total stranger?"

"It could be one of her old friends from Canada. Do you know anything else?"

"I spent some time on the computer. There's a man named Joel Martin who graduated from the University of British Columbia with a degree in Marine Biology. He teaches at the University. He's about the right age."

"That's not much. A man named Joel came to pay his respects. That's all. This is one of those things you might have to turn over."

"My mother is a liar and I have a half brother. Maybe he's dead, but it's *too big* to turn over."

Ida worked the night shift on Sunday, and Danny left the house early with Jedi for a morning visiting at the hospital. They spent the afternoon at a training center for therapy dogs, and Danny came in the house quietly, expecting Ida to still be asleep. He heated some soup, made a vegetarian omelet, and set the table. He opened the bedroom door to wake Ida for dinner, but the bed was empty. He looked around for a note. Then he dialed her cell phone, but it went directly to voicemail. "Hey, where are you? Dinner's ready."

Danny ate alone, fed ER and Jedi, and paced the living room as he tried to focus on a movie. He left several messages. He looked again throughout the house for a note, and that's when he discovered that two suitcases were missing, a black roller bag and a heavy roller duffle. Had she just up and left? Danny called her work. They said Ida was on vacation. None of her friends had heard anything. Jeff and Junior hadn't heard from her. There was no sign of Ida. He got on the computer and checked their bank accounts. She had written a check for $2,000 cash that day.

The night before, she and Danny had made love late into the night. Though their bodies were close, Danny felt agitated and distant. Something was different. Ida's body was cool and she didn't smell the same. Her skin always gave off a jasmine and wood scent, a spicy blend that was warm and earthy. Ida's smell always calmed Danny—he called her aroma the essence of Ida—but tonight it had vanished. She smelled antiseptic, sterile, as though she had rubbed herself down with alcohol. Danny's eyes welled up at the thought of losing her.

He sent texts and left messages late into the night. Finally, he sent a text saying that if she didn't call by tomorrow night, he was going to call the police and report her as a missing person.

2

da leaned over the edge of the painted aluminum boat, gripped the rail with both hands, and stared into the flashing water, mesmerized by the sunlight and the idling diesel engine throbbing in the background. Suddenly, without warning, a huge black shape emerged, and all six tons of a killer whale splashed up to the boat, bumped the side, and shocked Ida from her reverie. Wide-eyed, she gasped, jumped back, and spit the cold, salty water from her mouth. The whale rolled over, waving his floppy pink five-foot-long penis, turned onto his side, and gazed deeply into her green eyes with his glistening black eye, a yearning, soulful stare, followed at once by the eerie cry of his life song, a squeaky sound muted by swirling blue waves, playful splashes, and the wind in her ears. The steady gaze of his huge dark eye pulled her in, making Ida feel captured, frail, and off balance. It was as if the whale had seized something mysterious inside her, something that lay behind any thought she had ever had, deep down, like the shadow of a hiding stranger. Ida had not felt much at all since she had read her mother's old letter—not with Danny, and certainly not with Doug—and now, five yards from a 22-foot Orca killer whale near the US border, she shivered, and her stomach tightened as though she had taken a breathtaking plunge into cold water. In that scary moment, she sensed her life stretching and pulling apart, the 36 years before his powerful gaze, and her life beginning that day.

"You're so lucky," the tour guide said. Beth Odem was a woman in her mid-fifties with bright blue eyes, short silver-gray hair, tan, weathered skin, and a lighthearted smile. She smelled like lavender and salt water. "I've been watching these whales most of my life and I've never seen J26 wave his penis and stare at a human like that before. He seemed fearless today. His eye actually glowed. Amazing. I think he likes you." She grinned, a compassionate look that could have come from an older sister.

Ida squeezed her hands together. "J26? That's his name?"

"Well, he goes by Mike. You can tell by the white spots on his dorsal fin. He's about twelve, one of the young males in the J-Pod. He's in what they call the J16 Matriline."

"He's bigger than my brother's pickup truck," Ida said, clutching her hands to her heart. "He's magnificent. Oh, look. Here come some more."

"Oh, that's his sister Alki; she's about eight, and their mother J16. Her name is Slick. She's almost thirty-six. They usually travel together—a remarkable family. Mike will stay with his mother until she dies—all the Orcas stay in their Matriline with their mothers." Beth handed Ida her binoculars. "Look at about two o'clock, three-hundred meters out. That tall, wavy dorsal fin is Ruffles, and he's probably traveling with his mother Granny. She's the oldest killer whale we know of, almost one hundred. Ruffles is the oldest male, about fifty-five. Oh, there she is, just to his right. See her fin?"

Ida watched through the binoculars for a while, and then, eyes wet and blurring, she sat down with her hands on her face, pink now from the wind and the sea spray.

Beth touched her shoulder. "Are you okay?"

Ida's cheeks were wet with tears. "I'm tired."

Beth gave her a handful of tissues. "When did you come to Victoria?"

Ida wiped her eyes. "Yesterday, I flew from Albuquerque to Seattle—then to Victoria. It was a long day."

"Travel wears me out too." Beth smiled. "Did you sleep?"

"No. I was restless all night. I got up early and came down to the harbor to check out the whale-watching boats. The captain said he had room for one more, so here I am."

"On vacation?"

"In a way. Excuse me, I'm going to use the bathroom."

Ida locked herself in the bathroom, sat on the toilet, wiped her face with tissue, and turned on her cell phone. The last text from Danny frightened her. She didn't need the police looking for her. She sent Danny a text: "I'm in Canada, I'm okay. Have to find him. Give me space."

Ida returned and sat down by Beth. "Actually, I'm here looking for someone, a professor from the University of British Columbia named Dr. Joel Martin. He studies killer whales. Have you ever heard of him?"

"No, sorry. I don't know the name." Beth pointed to the east. "There's a whale research base over there in Friday Harbor. It's on the other side of the San Juan Island. Someone there might know him."

Ida lifted the binoculars to her eyes. The breeze came from the west, and the waves were building. "I need to find him."

"Is he a friend?"

"No. Actually, I've never met him."

"I see."

"He was at my mother's funeral."

"He knew your mother?"

"That's what I'm trying to find out. The university said he was gone for the summer doing Orca research, and he couldn't be reached."

"When we go in, I'll find the number of the whale research office on San Juan Island."

Ida nodded her head, watching the horizon of flashing water and milky-blue skies recede from the back of the boat. She shivered and crossed her arms, tucking her hands in her armpits. She tried to comfort herself by imagining, one by one, the faces and the yearning eyes of the many men who had desired her. But a gap was opening behind her, and her memories were fading, harder to hold, and strange things were happening. Last night, sleepless, she was surprised when she glanced into the bathroom mirror, and for some reason she didn't understand, she saw her mother's face appear in the shadowy sink—a twisted, dark face. Suddenly, a bright fear arose—the fabric wrapping her mind together began thinning and might easily tear. For the first time in a long time, panic arose, like a small child lost in a strange place. Maybe this trip was a fool's errand. Maybe she couldn't handle it. Maybe she was simply losing her mind.

The boat slowed down and turned. Ida took a breath and stood up. "What's happening now?"

"The captain's going to move us closer to Turn Point," Beth said, "so you need to stay seated."

"Sure," Ida said. She pointed. "Is that the US?" The wind fluttered the sleeve on her blue windbreaker.

"Yes, you can see San Juan Island and the top of Orcas Island in the background. We're headed to that lighthouse over there. That's Turn Point, the place where the ships turn that are coming out of Boundary Pass."

"Do the killer whales stay around?"

"We have a group of about eighty-five that stick around pretty close."

"They live here?"

"There's a group called the Southern Residents. They travel the Georgia Strait and the San Juan Islands."

Ida looked through the binoculars and swept the horizon. "I think I see a whale-watching boat way over there." She was enjoying Beth's teaching.

"That boat is probably out of Friday Harbor. Sometimes people go to the Lime Kiln Park and watch whales from the shore, over there, to your right. You can listen to them too."

"Listen to them?"

"They have hydrophones in the water near where they travel. Different groups make different sounds."

"Can they talk to each other?"

"They talk to each other all the time, real motor-mouths—they use echolocation to find food, like bats, and their squeaks and musical cries are their language."

"And you know all their names?"

Beth laughed. "Well, I don't. But they've all been identified by the different shapes of their dorsal fins and the white saddles on their backs." She took a brochure from her pocket. "Here's some photos—see, here's J16, the mother called Slick. J26 is her son Mike, and J36 is his sister Alki."

Ida took a breath. Her cheeks flushed. "This is incredible. I had no idea."

Beth pointed. "The US border is about two hundred meters over there in the water. We'll stay west of Turn Point, so we'll still be in Canada, but the whales will be back and forth. They fish for salmon there."

Ida laughed. "I guess the whales don't worry about boundaries."

Beth smiled. "They pretty much go where they want."

"How did you learn so much about Orcas? Are you a biologist?"

"It's sort of a hobby. I got involved when Greenpeace came to

Vancouver, twenty-five years ago. I helped my husband with save-the-whales efforts. There's something about the Orcas that captivates me. It sounds silly, but they've been around for ten thousand years, and I think they have things to teach us about how to live. Oh, we're slowing down. Let's go inside and I'll show you the map."

Ida and Beth stood by a large laminated map on the wall, and Beth traced the boat's course and the yellow line in the ocean that marked the Canadian-US border. She showed Ida the range of the 200 or so northern residents up Johnstone Strait by Alert Bay and on to Alaska; then traced her hand on the west side of Vancouver Island, south around the San Juan Islands, and back north past Victoria and Sidney, showing Ida the range of the 85 southern residents.

"When did you move to Victoria?" Ida asked.

"This is my second summer."

"To work on the whale-watching boat?"

Beth crossed her arms and gazed up at the clouds, eyes welling up. "No, my husband died—colon cancer—and I needed a change."

"I'm sorry."

"I'm a social worker, work for the government with family placement and assistance—domestic issues. I took a leave of absence."

The boat turned slightly and slowed to an idle. The captain stuck his head out the window of the pilothouse. "Whales on the starboard bow."

A procession of a dozen whales frolicked by about 100 meters out. "It's the K pod," Beth said, "and they're moving fast, probably about ten kilo... Six miles per hour." Cameras clicked all around Ida. She felt exhilarated, recalling Mike's dark eye and his whale song. That moment brightened, reappearing in a shimmer, rising up in the sunny mist of whales blowing. She shivered.

As they tied up and began stepping off the boat, Ida turned to Beth, grabbing her arm, holding on. "Could I treat you to dinner? I have no idea where to eat—I don't know what's next."

Beth smiled. "I'm scheduled for a class this evening, but I'm free tomorrow."

"Let's meet about six—say at the tourist information area?"

"Sure. See you tomorrow night."

3

da inhaled a deep breath of cool Canadian air, walked back to her room at the Empress Hotel, and then went to the bar, dressed in black tights, a long white sweater with a green belt, and her ponytail tied with a green scarf. She put her small shoulder bag on the bar as she slid up on a stool.

"What's your pleasure missy?" the bartender asked. He was twice Ida's age, had wavy, white hair, and smiled from under a reddish nose and droopy gray eyes that had seen too much.

"Gin and tonic, please." Ida smiled, folding her hands on the bar.

"Coming up. On vacation?"

"In a way."

"By yourself?"

"Yes, but actually I'm looking for someone, my half brother."

The bartender put the glass in front of Ida and grinned. "I could be him if you'd like, and if I were thirty years younger."

"Have you ever heard of Professor Joel Martin? He's a whale biologist from UBC."

"Is he your half brother?"

"Maybe."

The bartender tipped his head. "Can't say as I have."

"How long have you worked here?"

"Twenty years. Came to work here off a fishing boat in eighty-three." He put his hands behind him, straightening up. "I've got a bad back—have to wear a brace."

"Sorry." Ida reached into her purse and placed the old coaster carefully on the bar. "Have you ever seen a coaster like this one?"

The bartender took it and held it up to a light. "That's an old one, before my time. That sketch is the Empress all right, back before the addition."

"You sure it is this Empress Hotel?"

He pointed over Ida's head. "Look over there on the wall. Those are artist sketches from over the years. See, there's the one on the coaster, right there on the end, bottom row."

Ida carried her drink as she walked along the wall slowly, looking at the dozen sketches. The one that matched the coaster was a pen and ink sketch, about two feet square, signed with a date of 1959.

"That's the one, right, missy?"

Ida sat down and drained her drink. "Yes. I think it is around the time he was born. Mom must have been here. Why else would she keep the coaster?"

"I don't know, missy. People like souvenirs."

Ida sat silently and had four more drinks trying to piece things together. Maybe Mom and Grandmother Hawthorn stayed here together? Could he have been born in a hotel? No, it was more secret than that. Joel must have been born at someone's house, maybe attended by a midwife. Somehow, he got a birth certificate. Maybe his adoptive parents had a doctor friend write one. Where did he live all these years? He must have known—he came to Mom's memorial service. How did he know she died?

Ida's mind clouded over as she staggered to her room, flopped down on the bed fully clothed, and slept fitfully, flashes of hospital workers dressed in white, and smells of dirty gray mop water running through her jumbled dreams.

It was late afternoon when Ida awoke with a raging headache. She undressed, took four aspirin, and stepped in the shower, letting the hot water run over her head and down her back for a long time. *Why did I drink so much?*

As Ida dressed and dried her hair, she could not stop the tremors in her hands. She dressed in new blue jeans, a light blue mock turtleneck jersey shirt, and tied her hair back in a tight ponytail with a blue scarf. She went to the restaurant, drank coffee, and picked at an order of fish and chips as she read the real estate ads in the newspaper. She had missed reservations for High Tea, but found an opening at the spa and went in for a manicure and pedicure. She charged the bill to her room, put on her dark blue windbreaker, and walked through the downtown area, looking at clothes, following a tourist map. She walked up Government to Fort, and went into Munro's bookstore, a legend in Victoria for over forty years. It was called "one of the bookstores you must see before you die." She went straight to the first editions and started browsing. They had one first edition, signed copy of Margaret Atwood's *The Handmaid's Tale* with a fair-to-good book jacket. The clerk opened the glass case and handed Ida the book. The dust jacket was protected with a plastic cover. The back was faded, and there were a few small tears. Still, $95 Canadian seemed like a good price. On the same shelf, she spied a copy of Jonis Agee's *Mercury, A Short Story*. It was bound in boards, signed by the author and the illustrator, and was in fine condition, tucked inside a heavy plastic envelope, marked $40. She took it out, felt the texture of the boards, and admired the clear signatures. She handed the clerk her Visa card and bought them both. She crossed the street, bought an espresso and a biscuit, and sat outside under a table umbrella. Victoria was busy with tourists, and Ida watched people walk by—couples holding hands—imagining what their lives must be like, imagining that they had planned their vacations together around dining room tables, found peace of mind in each other's company, looked forward to sex in a hotel bed, could fall asleep easily afterward, knew the birthdays of their nieces and nephews, and were eager for the next holiday gathering. Ida finished her espresso and walked back down Government to Victoria Harbor, pausing to watch a juggler with flaming torches, just as dusk crept in on the dreary flood tide. The black batons of orange fire swooshed rhythmically against the gray sky, giving off the pungent odor of smoke and lighter fluid. Ida was mesmerized, her eyes following the tumbling flames, shimmering, reminding her of the flashes of light in the killer whale's black eye. Had she been taken in, somehow captured by Mike's eye? The fire seemed to be a complete circle, one torch flickering away as the next one took its place, as if a flaming wheel of fire surrounded the juggler's beaming face and enclosed him with warmth and light. Ida welled up, swallowing a crampy lump in her throat. What was happening? Beth walked up dressed in dark slacks and a green sweater. "Are you hungry?"

Ida jumped, then smiled, touching her hand to her stomach. "You surprised me. Yes, I'm ready to eat. Have you picked out a place?"

"I made reservations over at the Harbor House. I hope you like seafood, because they've got the best. We can walk. Let's go this way."

They were seated, and the waiter brought water and a wine list. "The house Chardonnay is quite good," Beth said. "Would you like a glass?"

"Sure."

The wine came, and Beth held her glass for Ida's glass to touch. "Cheers."

"Where are you staying?" Beth asked.

"At the Empress. I think my mother and grandmother stayed there years ago."

"Wow. Elegant. I guess you know they serve High Tea. It's a big deal with little crumpets and cakes, and people dress for it. Some people on the boat yesterday said they had to make reservations two months in advance."

Ida finished her wine. "Too fancy for me. I decided to go to the spa." She held up her hand showing Beth her nails.

They both ordered the crab cakes, and the waiter filled their wine glasses.

Beth raised her glass. "Cheers." They touched glasses and smiled as they sipped the wine.

Beth handed Ida a slip of paper. "Here's the phone number to the whale research center. So tell me, who is this Dr. Joel Martin, and why exactly are you looking for him?"

Ida looked down at her plate.

"You said he came to your mother's funeral?"

"Yes. I recently discovered I have a half brother."

"Joel Martin might be him?"

"He's eight years older than me, but I've never met him."

Beth leaned forward. "Do you think he's in Victoria?"

"Oh, probably not. It seemed like a good place to start. In Mother's things I found an old cork coaster from the Empress. I'm pretty sure she stayed there when she was pregnant."

"So you think he was born here?"

Ida gulped some wine and gritted her teeth. "My mother gave him away to a Canadian couple when he was born, friends of my grandmother. That's what the letter said. My guess is he was born in their house."

"Letter?"

"My mother died two years ago in July. I finally got up the nerve to go through some of her things, and found a love letter from someone named Fred. A few days before she passed away, she told me she had an abortion, but it turns out she didn't—she had the baby and gave it away. My grandmother Hawthorn had some friends here."

Beth moved the bread as their dinners arrived. "So this surprise has, well, set you back?"

Ida crossed her hands over her heart. "My mother lied to me. She lied to me just before she died. Can you believe she would lie to me on her deathbed?"

They were both quiet for a few minutes as they sampled everything on their plates. The crab cakes came with roasted red potato slices, asparagus, and a lemon-based coleslaw.

Ida signaled for more wine with her empty glass.

"I'm sorry, losing your mother and then finding out you have a brother—that's got to be tough. I'm still shaky from my husband's death. The government gave me bereavement leave for three months, but then I had to take a leave of absence. Fortunately, I've had the same job for twenty-five years, so I'll be able to go back. The government's good about those things."

"Where did you work?"

"I transferred to Vancouver when my husband got sick. That's where he got his treatments. Before that, we lived here on Vancouver Island—north of here past Parksville—in Qualicum Beach. I worked up and down the island, mostly small towns. My husband was a biologist and worked at the salmon hatchery."

"Did you ever meet people from the University of British Columbia?"

"That's where I went to school. I have my Social Work degree from UBC. But that was thirty years ago. Heavens, I'm sure I've forgotten more people than I remember."

Ida took a breath. "A strange man came to my mother's memorial service at the church and signed in as Joel Martin from Victoria. That's got to mean something."

"That does seem odd."

"I found a Professor Joel Martin at the UBC. He's a marine biologist, like I said, and specializes in killer whales—ah, Orcas—so that's why I went whale-watching. You sure you haven't heard of him?"

"Sorry. I know most of the people that work on the whale-watching boats. We can ask around in the morning. I know someone in Friday Harbor. She can check with volunteers at the Center for Whale Research. I'll email her, and you can call over there."

"Thanks. That would be great."

"Meet me at the boat at about seven am and we can talk with crewmembers."

Beth and Ida drank another bottle of wine and talked late into the evening. When they left the restaurant, they were arm in arm, laughing. Ida told Beth good night, made her way to her room in the Empress, and slept through the night. She answered the wake-up call at 5:30 am, showered, dressed in blue jeans, white tennis shoes, and a green sweater. She pulled her hair up in a ponytail and put it through the back of a new white cap that said "Victoria, BC," and grabbed her blue windbreaker. After a sweet roll and coffee, she walked to the harbor and found Beth by the whale-watching boat. She was washing the windshield of the pilothouse. "I'll be right down."

"Take your time," Ida said. It started raining lightly, so Ida pulled her hood up over her hat.

Beth hopped down. "Come on, let's go this way."

They stopped at every whale-watching boat and ticket office in Victoria Harbor, but no one had heard of Dr. Joel Martin. One captain said that most of the research was either around the San Juan Islands or up near Alert Bay on Cormorant Island. "There's a lot of whale-watching up north. That's where I would go."

"Come on out with me," Beth said. "It'll do you good to see some more whales. We can talk some more."

Ida's shoulders slumped. "Okay. I don't want to spend a day walking around. It's too cold and rainy."

Later, on the way back to the dock at the end of the day, Beth took Ida's hands, smiling brightly. "I'm off for a couple of days. Would you like to come home with me? I have room."

Ida turned her face to the misty rain.

"I'd like that. I don't like being alone. Can you tell?"

"I understand when people are in difficult times. You look like you need a friend."

"Thanks. I'm not sure what to do next."

"Go check out of the hotel and I'll pick you up at the front in an hour."

Ida packed quickly, checked out at the front desk, and walked out the door just as Beth drove up in her old white Volvo. She helped Ida put her backpack and roller bag in the backseat.

"My house is not far from here."

"Are you in a neighborhood?"

"Sort of. It's a RV park. I have a thirty-two-foot motor home and rent a space for the summer."

"By the water?"

"Yes, it's right by the water. Oceanside RV Resort, about twenty kilometers from here. We go north on the Pacific Bay Highway. It's a nice drive."

They were quiet except for Beth pointing out scenic places. The rain had stopped, and the sun made the little waves sparkle. "There are beautiful home along here," Ida said. "Looks pricey."

"They're way beyond my means, but I'm close to the water, and I have a couple of kayaks, so we can see the same things these rich folks see." She slowed down and turned right at the Mt. Newton Cross Road. They pulled up to the Oceanside RV Resort and made their way to a spot near the back. Beth parked by the door.

"Here we are." She opened the door, and they moved Ida's things inside. Ida noticed two kayaks under the motor home, both bright yellow. One was a double.

"I know it feels small," Beth said, "but it's quite efficient." She climbed up a short ladder. "I'll just pull your bed down."

Beth's motor home was clean and tidy, and featured a small fold-down dinette, a galley kitchen, a bathroom, and a bedroom in the back. Ida's bed was above the driver's seat.

"Would you like some tea?" Beth said. She turned on a burner and put on the kettle.

"Sure, that would be great. This is a nice place. Thank you for your hospitality."

After tea, they went for a walk along the shore. Beth pointed. "The closest land is James Island. Just past that is Sidney Island, and in the distance you can see the Turn Point on Stuart Island. That's where we stopped for a while and saw the K Pod."

"What's that little island to the right?"

"D'Arcy, and right behind it is Little D'Arcy. You can't see it from here."

"It's beautiful. Oh Beth, I feel so lost."

"I know. I'm sorry."

"Do you get cell phone service here? I feel like calling Danny."

"Yes, the Victoria area has good coverage. You'll be roaming, though."

They walked back to the motor home. Ida filled her teacup, and then sat down outside at a picnic table. She dialed Danny's number.

"Sweetheart, is everything okay?"

"I went on a whale-watching boat yesterday. A whale named Mike came right up to me, like we were friends. It was astounding."

"A whale named Mike? Are you drinking?"

"No, all the Orca killer whales around here have names and numbers. They live here."

"Any leads on finding that guy Joel what's-his-name?"

"Joel Martin. I met a tour guide—Beth. We asked around the docks in the Victoria Harbor, and no one has heard of him. The University said he was out on a research project for the summer."

"Any idea where?"

"No. I'm pretty down about it, but Beth invited me to stay at her house. It's close to the water."

"It sounds like a wild goose chase."

"I've got to keep looking, Danny. I need space and I need your support."

"You're going to get more disappointed. There's no telling where he is, and you don't know anything about him. Come home. Take it from me, this can't have a good ending."

Ida held the phone out in front of her and frowned. "Bye." She hung up, stuffed her phone into her pocket.

Beth and Ida talked until late and went to bed around midnight. Ida slept until four am, and then awoke with a start. She had been dreaming about Mom as a teenager, a pregnant young girl hiding out, covering her stomach with bulky clothes, afraid to go out of the house. Ida climbed down the ladder and sat down by the window with a glass of water. As she rotated the glass on the table, moonlight sparkled in the water. Ida put her chin on her hands and made herself stare at the glass, hoping to quiet the angry ghosts swirling in her mind, staccato pulses that bounced off the inside of her forehead. A deep pain surged behind her eyes, and she slapped the glass off the table, pounding her fist.

Beth quietly walked up and sat down beside her. "I'm worried about you. Can I help?"

"I'm losing it. Danny wants me to come home. This has got me twisted up in knots."

"Let's relax for a few days. I sent out emails. The whale community is tight, so word will get around soon. Let's have breakfast and go kayaking. I think it will be calm this morning."

Ida took a deep breath and stood up. "I've never done that. Will you show me?"

"Sure. I'll make coffee and some eggs. You make some toast—there's cinnamon bread in the fridge."

After breakfast, Ida called the Whale Research Center number and left a message. She did the dishes as Beth dug around and pulled kayaking gear out of the closet. They dressed in tights, camping pants, and rain jackets. Beth handed Ida some rubber booties. "Here, try these on. They're good for walking on the beach and in the water."

Beth put the bow of the double kayak on a rack with small wheels. They lifted the stern with handles on a rope, and eased the kayak down the trail to the water. Beth held it still while Ida practiced getting in and out, adjusting the seat, and zipping up the cover. They strapped down water bottles, and Beth pushed a dry bag into a compartment. She handed Ida a brimmed hat, pushed the kayak out, and sat gracefully on the back, slipping into her seat. "Okay, now paddle slowly until you get used to the balance. I'll take care of steering."

"This is incredible. We're right next to the water."

Beth laughed. "I love it too. You can stop paddling. The tide is ebbing, so it will pull us out. We'll head over to Henry Island. It's only about one and a half kilometers."

The sun was warm, and the water was calm. There were a few waves from the boats in the distance. Ida pointed. "Is that the ferry?"

"Yes, that's the ferry from Anacortes to Sidney. We'll get some waves in about fifteen minutes."

As they approached the southern tip of Henry Island, Beth said, "Check it out. Here come the waves from the ferry." They bounced a few times, and water splashed on Ida's face. "This is great."

Beth found a sandy spot where they could come ashore, and paddled straight for it until they hit bottom. She slipped out, stood in the water, and steadied the kayak. "I'll hold it." Ida fumbled and giggled getting out, and then they pulled the kayak up on dry ground. Beth grabbed the dry bag and their water bottles. "Come on. There's a place by those logs where we can sit for a while. You can find a place to pee behind those trees."

They took off their life jackets, settled down on a gray driftwood log, and Beth reached in the bag. "I brought some snacks." She offered Ida an apple and a muffin. They ate slowly in the quiet breeze, watching the birds and listening to the gentle waves. Ida found a spot where she could lie back on the sand and soon fell into a half sleep, hypnagogic images floating by, little clouds, sun rays, bird sounds, and the smell of salty air.

Ida sat up straight. "Whoa, what time is it?"

"It's about three o'clock. You must have needed the sleep."

"This place, the water, the sun—it's magical."

"Ready to head back?"

"In a minute." Ida went into the trees and returned, buttoning her pants. "That's better. I'm ready now."

They launched the kayak and paddled out. "Let's take it easy. We're almost at slack tide, and soon the flood tide will help us home."

Back in the motor home, they each took showers and dressed in fresh clothes. Ida's face was pink from the sun, and her blond hair was radiant from the conditioner.

"Shall we go out or cook here?" Beth asked.

"Let's just stay here. It's been such a beautiful day."

"Sure. I'll make some pasta with salmon, and we can eat at the picnic table. It won't get dark until later, and we can have ice cream in the gloaming."

"The gloaming?"

"The time after sunset and before dark—when the world changes. We call that the gloaming. Maybe you call it twilight or dusk."

They sat at the table, and Ida talked nonstop for an hour about Mom's death, her brothers, her relationship with Danny, and the drama of the past year. Beth listened patiently, offering comfort when Ida welled up, and then she talked about her husband dying in the hospice wing of the hospital, and how his pain could not be stopped. "He died in pain. He couldn't even recognize I was holding his hand."

The sun went down over the horizon at about nine pm, casting orange and pink flashes against the drifting clouds. Beth went to the refrigerator and dished out two bowls of chocolate swirl. They sat quietly eating ice cream, listening to the sounds of the water and the night coming in, rustles and chirps, the hoot of an owl, and a gentle breeze carrying the pungent scent of fir trees.

In the morning, Beth scrolled through her email. Several people had heard of Dr. Joel Martin from his journal articles about Orcas, but no one knew him. "I'm sorry, but no one has any information. One friend cited an article of Martin's, but it's a couple years old—about the short life span of captured Orcas. Nothing about research in this area."

Ida bit her lip. "Any ideas?"

"I was thinking we could drive up to the ferry dock and ask the crew, but that's a long shot. Then we could walk around the marina at Port Sidney and inquire."

Ida took a deep breath and let it out slowly, shaking her head.

Beth hugged her. "Come on, let's head out in the kayak. It'll do you good."

They packed food, water, and raingear, launched the kayak, and headed out toward Sidney Island. "It's only about five kilometers," Beth said. "The tide's helping, so we'll be there in a couple of easy hours."

They paddled quietly, rocking on gentle waves and watching the sun hide behind the passing clouds. Gulls floated overhead, hoping for a snack. The sound of the breeze from the south and dripping water from their paddles filled Ida's mind. Time passed quickly, and soon Beth turned them to the southeastern shoreline of Sidney Island. They landed, pulled the kayak up, and found a shady spot under an old cedar tree. The crisp, woody smell of the tree and the salt air filled Ida's lungs, and a little smile appeared on her mouth. "This is beautiful. I could sit here forever."

Beth touched her arm. "Summers are great here, beginning a couple of weeks ago. July and August are even better. They call Sidney Island 'the jewel of the Gulf Islands'—mostly undeveloped."

Ida laid her head down on her life jacket and snoozed. She awoke to the sounds of ravens cackling in the tree overhead. Beth was walking back along the shoreline. She waved and then beckoned. "Come on this way. I want to show you some very old fir trees."

They wandered slowly through the trees. "There, isn't that magnificent? It's old growth—no one has logged around here." They both leaned back, looking up the tree, fascinated.

"It's so old and stable—can we camp overnight?" Ida asked.

"We shouldn't here, but we can paddle around to the north side. There's a campground there. It's actually quite nice."

Ida sighed. "Maybe another time."

They meandered around on the island for a couple of hours, had some dinner of cheddar cheese, graham crackers, and apples, and then packed up and got ready to go. "It's about seven thirty. We'd better start back," Beth said. "We'll catch the tide going in, but it's still a couple of hours to get home."

"How long does it stay light?"

"Until nine or so—but we can still see for a while in the gloaming. It's not cloudy, and there's a half-moon tonight."

"The gloaming—that's beautiful. It sounds so alluring, like a mysterious place."

"Some say it's another reality." Beth touched Ida's arm. "You know, a shadow land, a place where spirits and night creatures begin to stir."

"Spirits?"

"Yes, spirits, but I think that's just a word for another place—you know, that place beyond our senses where everything is connected."

"No, I don't know."

They paddled quietly, watching the yellow-orange sunset behind the trees and coasting along with the incoming tide. They passed some small rocky islands on their right, paddled steadily for another 20 minutes, and then rested. Ida saw the distant lights come on in the RV resort and then heard a sharp whoosh of air behind her, then two more blows. "Be still," Beth said. "Orca whales just surfaced. Oh good Lord, there are three of them—only twenty meters out." Beth turned the kayak, and Ida saw three smooth, black humps and three dorsal fins, one almost six feet tall. They blew loudly, in unison. "Is that Mike?"

"It is. Alki and Slick are there beside him—this is incredible."

Ida held her breath, mouth open, and heart pounding like a bass drum inside her chest. She shifted in her seat.

Mike approached slowly—20 meters, then 10 meters, then three meters—his dark eye glistening in the shadowy light, catching and holding Ida's gaze for 10 or 12 heartbeats. Quietly he dove, and within 15 seconds, he breeched about 30 meters in front of the kayak, came down with a huge splash, and then dove again. Ida counted 10 quick heartbeats, and a third of Mike's body rushed straight up out of the water head first, just five meters ahead, and then dropped, the rising half-moon luminous on his white belly. "That's spyhopping," Beth said, breathless, as the kayak rocked, water flowing over the bow. "He's checking us out." Alki and Slick rested on the surface, their blowing making a rhythmic sound, a misty duet against the fading sky. Mike spyhopped again, then dove, then came up sideways, slapping the water sharply with his right pectoral fin. Beth steadied the kayak from the waves. "That's a fin slap. He's really putting on a show."

Ida sat very still, wide-eyed, gripping her paddle with both hands, her stomach fluttering, taking deep breaths of misty air. A wave from Mike's slap splashed water over the side of the kayak, spraying her face. She watched the water race over the yellow hull, and then licked her lips, tasting the crisp salt of the cool sea.

Mike dove again, came up closer, waved, and then slapped his right fin again, as though he was urging Ida to follow him. "Come on," he seemed to say. Then Ida felt a strange drumming in her mind, a steady cadence that matched her heartbeat, thump for thump. Suddenly a clear, bright thought arose, a huge thought bubble that filled her up from head to toe and seemed to shout, "Go north."

She balanced her paddle carefully across the kayak and held her head in her hands, covering her ears, squeezing her eyes shut, and shaking her head. "Go north," her mind shouted, the words clanging like symbols. She shivered and looked up in time to see Mike, Slick, and Alki dive together and then surface 30 meters ahead, then again at 50 meters, until they began to disappear like apparitions into the gloaming. Transfixed, Ida watched what seemed like shadowy feelings bubble up from the dark, distant water, and then skip along the top toward her, making quick little flashes in the emerging moonlight—Mike's warm feelings touching her tepid ones, making her shiver uncontrollably, a swirling blend of feelings from his heart and hers, formed by some deep, mysterious force. Ida held her breath, weeping. "North," she whispered.

Beth shook her head, paddled slowly, and turned them toward the shore. "Astonishing—I've *never* seen anything like this."

"Mike *told me* to go north," Ida said, wiping her eyes. "He said it plain as day, in my mind. I know it was him."

"He told you?"

"Yes, he told me all over me, in my head, in my body—everywhere."

Beth paddled quietly. "Do you believe in mental telepathy?"

Ida turned her head and looked back. "Telepathy?"

4

eth switched off the slapping windshield wipers as she parked her Volvo across the street from the Port Sidney Marina office. Ida tightened the strap on her floppy rain hat, and slipped out of the car. They walked quickly through the office door as a middle-aged man in a Port Sidney cap looked up from behind a long counter covered with laminated maps. "Can I help you?"

Beth smiled and walked up to the counter. Ida took off her hat, shook out her hair, and then tied it into a loose ponytail. She looked around at the photos, walked up beside Beth, and smiled.

"Are you the one who schedules the transient moorage?" Beth asked.

"Sure, when I'm here. Are you in a boat?"

"No, we're looking for someone, and he may have stopped here."

"We have new boats every night. I don't know that I'd remember. Who are you looking for?"

"Joel Martin," Ida said. She unzipped her rain jacket. "He's a professor from UBC who's doing research on killer whales."

"I don't recall anyone by that name, but you're welcome to look at the guest moorage book." He opened a hardback journal on the counter. "This one goes back to March."

"Thank you," Ida said. She ran her finger down each page of names as she turned the pages. There were no Martins. She looked at Beth. "No leads here." She closed the book and slid it back across the counter. "Thanks."

The man pointed at the windows to the north. "We've got over three-hundred slips out there, and only a few vacancies. He might be staying with someone. Only boat owners are required to sign in."

"Come on," Beth said. "Let's go for a walk on the docks." She stopped, smiling at the man. "Is it okay for us to use your washroom?"

"Sure. Go out that door, down the stairs, and then turn right. The door code is seven-two-five-eight. We don't lock the gate to the slips until eight."

Beth and Ida went to the washroom and then walked down the ramp to the docks.

"What do we do now?" Ida asked.

"Let's walk along and see if we can find anyone. The gray day and the rain probably have a lot of people sitting around in their boats."

They strolled in the gentle rain out and back on the A, B, C, and D docks. On the way back on the D dock, about D-20, they saw an older woman with short silver-gray hair smoking under an open roof outside the back door of a large new trawler. The boat was moored with the stern at the dock. She was dressed in jeans, a blue hooded sweatshirt, and stood about 5' 8" tall between a large pot of yellow daisy chrysanthemums and another pot of mixed pink and purple petunias. She had one arm crossed over the other, and between two fingers, she held the cigarette next to her pursed mouth and bony chin. Her wrinkled forehead was drawn down, as though an invisible fishing line pulled her head toward her knees.

"I promised my husband I wouldn't smoke in the boat," she said as Beth and Ida stopped. "It's brand new. He says it's our retirement dream. We're supposed to be on our maiden voyage around the island, but my husband hurt his foot, so we're waiting until he gets better."

"How long have you been here in the harbor?" Beth asked.

"Almost a month, now." She tossed the cigarette into the water, offering a gentle smile. "My name is Dorothy," she said, "Dorothy McHugh."

Beth stepped closer. "I'm Beth Odem, and this is Ida Corley. We're looking for someone."

"Come aboard. Get out of the rain." Dorothy swung open a three-foot transom door, and they stepped aboard under the roof. "Sit down if you'd like." She motioned to a couple of folding deck chairs. "Would you like some hot tea? I've got the kettle on."

"Sure," Ida said, sitting down, shaking out her rain hat. "That would be great."

Dorothy slid open the door, stepped to the galley, and returned quickly with three cups of tea. "I put sugar and milk in all of them. A habit. Hope that's okay."

Ida sipped her tea. "We're looking for a professor from UBC who does killer whale research. His name is Joel Martin, and they say he's somewhere around Vancouver Island. Have you heard of anyone like that?"

"No, I don't think so. Is he a friend?"

Ida balanced her cup on her thigh and crossed her arms. Her mouth shaped into a pout. "No, I've never met him."

"Where are you from?"

"Albuquerque, New Mexico."

"Wow, that's a long way away. And you think he's in BC?"

"I only have one lead. He signed in at my mother's funeral about two years ago. No one had heard of him before. My mother told me she had an abortion when she was young, but I found out that she had a boy and gave him away to some friends on Vancouver Island. It might be him. That's all I know."

Dorothy's eyebrows furrowed. "When did you find out?

"A couple of months ago. I found an old love letter to Mom when she was a teenager."

"Sorry, I don't mean to be so nosy. I wish I had seen him so I could be more helpful."

Beth looked over her shoulder. A short, ruddy-faced man with bushy white eyebrows and a white beard was coming down the dock, walking with crutches. A dockhand walked behind him, pulling a cart covered with a blue tarp. Dorothy stood up. "That's my husband, Paul. He's been to the grocery store."

Ida and Beth stood up, out of the way, as Paul balanced on one crutch and began handing plastic grocery bags through the transom door. He smiled from a round face and looked at them with a wry smile. He smelled like wet clothes and wine. "Hope you don't mind grabbing these," he said. "I'm Paul McHugh, and right now, I've got to get these groceries out of the weather." Looking through glazed eyes, he handed off bags to reaching hands.

Ida, Beth, and Dorothy put the bags on the deck near the door. Paul motioned to the dockhand, and he put two cases of wine on the deck, both mixed red Averill Creek Prevost. Paul handed off the last of the bags and fished in his pocket for a tip. The dockhand hurried back up to the building as Paul hopped aboard, crutch first. It was crowded under the canopy. "Come on in," Paul said. "I'll show you around. Welcome to the good ship *Destiny*."

He went in, leaning on a light green Corian countertop, and waved his hand around the cabin. "All this teakwood is from the same tree. See how it matches? Even the floor."

Ida looked around at the full galley, the cabinets, furnishings, array of windows, and stairways up and down. Wine glasses hung from a rack on the ceiling in the galley, and teak handles lined the ceiling's centerline, handholds while walking through the cabin.

Paul hopped with one crutch to the six stairs on the starboard side. "Check up here. This is the pilothouse." He held the railing and hopped up the stairs. Ida followed. An array of controls and a couple of screens took up the center of the built-in platform, maps strewn along the sides. A large chrome steering wheel was fixed vertically in the center, ahead of a leather captain's chair. To the rear, there was a five-foot cushion at chair height. Teak trim surrounded two sliding doors, one on each side. Paul stood with his hand on the wheel, red face beaming, white eyebrows moving up and down like creeping caterpillars.

"This is beautiful," Ida said. She touched the smooth teak railing. Beth stood on the stairs, peering around, her hand at her mouth.

"Come on, I'll show you downstairs." Paul clumped along ahead of them, turning and hopping down three stairs in the center. He pointed left. "Here's the portside cabin. Small, but room for two good friends." Then to the right. "Here's the head. It's got a shower, and the toilet is a vacuflush."

He moved forward, sliding open a door. "And check this out—the master bedroom." He moved to one side as Ida and Beth looked in. Cabinets and shelves lined the walls, and the huge bed was centered, fluffy cushions piled at the bow. Paul squeezed by, and dropped to his knees in the hallway. He lifted up the three stairs that were hinged at the back, reached down, and snapped on a light. "Here's the engine room. It's a 370 horsepower Cummins diesel." Ida looked over his shoulder at a huge engine painted a brilliant white. Four plastic storage tubs held filters, tools, oil, and spare hoses and parts. The engine area was spotless. He swung the stairs down and then pushed a throw rug aside near the galley. "There's another access," he said, flipping the handles up and down. "You just take up this part of the floor. What do you think, eh?"

Beth and Ida both raised their eyebrows, moving to the built-in seat. Dorothy had served two fresh cups of tea and put them on cork coasters decorated with Canadian flags. Wide-eyed, Ida sipped her tea and gazed around at the light green curtains and matching cushions. *Incredible craftsmanship—I wish I could show Danny.*

Paul sat on a stool and leaned back, arm on the counter. "Now what brings you to Sidney?"

"They're looking for someone," Dorothy said, "a man named Joel Martin, a professor from UBC."

Paul smiled. "Haven't seen any loose professors around here. What does he teach?"

"Marine biology," Ida said. "He does research on killer whales."

"Sorry, I haven't heard of him. Is he supposed to be around here?"

"At the university they said he was somewhere around Vancouver Island on a research project."

"I told them to come back tomorrow," Dorothy said. "The weather's supposed to be good, and we can introduce them around the marina. Maybe someone has heard of him."

Ida and Beth stood up, walking to the doorway. "Thank you so much," Beth said, "we'll come back tomorrow after lunch." They shook hands all around, walked quickly to the car, and drove back to Beth's house.

"Let's walk downtown," Ida said. "There's a bookstore here I want to check out."

"Sure. We can get a sandwich, and there's a Roger's Chocolate Store."

They made their way to Beacon Street and headed west. Beth pulled Ida's sleeve and they ducked into Miss Bliss Boutique and looked at some leather bags. Then they sampled chocolate in Roger's and ended up buying a supply of dark chocolate and raspberry drops.

"The Beacon Street Bookstore is just over there," Ida said. "I want to check out the first editions."

"I'm going to walk on back to the Stonestreet Café. I'll wait for you there and we can have a sandwich."

Ida found her way to the rare book section. This would be an opportunity to look for something by Alice Munro—her favorite Canadian author. Two titles jumped out at her, *Love of a Good Woman* and *Too Much Happiness*, each first editions, signed, and in good to fine condition. She decided on *Too Much Happiness* for $140 Canadian. She paid the extra $15 to have it shipped to her in care of her father. She didn't need to carry books around.

Ida stepped outside and called Danny. He answered on the second ring.

"How are you?"

"I'm fine. I'm in Sidney. Met some people at the marina."

"Sidney? Why did you go there?"

"You're not going to believe this, but I'm sure I need to go further north."

"You're sure?"

"Yes. We were out in kayaks and I saw the whales again. It was incredible. I kept getting the feeling I should keep searching."

"A feeling?"

"An intuition or something—Beth said maybe it was mental telepathy, but I felt it all over."

"Sounds like you want to feel that way."

"Maybe so, but the feeling came from Mike."

"Mike the killer whale?"

"Yes."

There was a long pause.

"Ida, are you all right? Are you sleeping?"

Ida rolled her eyes. "Of course. I'm doing fine."

"Do you have any real clues about Martin?"

"No, but these people, the McHughs, are going to introduce us around the marina tomorrow. Someone might have heard of him."

"The McHughs? Who are they?"

"Beth and I walked around the Port Sidney Marina, and we met them there. They live on a boat. Nice couple, retired. They're on a trip around Vancouver Island."

"This seems more and more like a wild goose chase. Can't you just come home?"

"No. I've got to do this. Please support me. I don't need any more conflict."

"I miss you a lot. The house seems so empty."

"You've got Jedi and ER. Let them get up in the bed. They're both good company."

"Not like you. This is getting hard. It seems so pointless. We've got a good life here."

Ida took a breath and gritted her teeth. "Got to go now. Bye."

When she came into the Stonestreet Cafe, her chin was down, and she was wiping tears from her cheeks.

"What is it?" Beth asked.

"Danny. He doesn't understand. You know what? I'm having second thoughts about this wedding."

oneliness ran deep in Danny's soul, and appeared on his face as a childish grin with curious eyes, a combination that somehow created a magnet for women who imagined themselves as caring and compassionate. The near-dalliance began with the yowling and forlorn baying of a dog named Brimley. Danny had begun teaching a new dog training class at Pet Smart when she walked up dragging a little beagle behind her by a red leather leash. "Am I too late for the class?"

Danny paused. "No, come in the gate over there and take a seat."

"Is this the beginning class?" She looked around. Ten other people sat in plastic chairs with dogs squirming by their sides, annoyed by her late arrival.

"Yes. This is the first of ten. It's eighty-five dollars for the series. You can make the check out to Danny Sandoval."

She quickly wrote out a check and handed it to him. The printed address said Doris Espinoza, but the signature was different. Danny held the check a moment and looked at her. "Doris Espinoza, is that right?"

"Yes, but everyone calls me Dusty." She smiled and held the beagle. "This is Brimley."

Danny looked her over. She was about 40, tall, tan, lean, and had short auburn hair with tousled bangs; her gray-green eyes made her look poised and strong. Maybe a runner or a tennis player. Brimley was intractable, more or less out of control, and quivered with anxiety. Danny groaned to himself. This would take patience.

She waited after the class so she could talk with Danny. "I'm desperate. Could you please come over and help? I'll pay extra for more lessons. The neighbors leave nasty messages on my recorder. I'm going to get fined. My apartment is a mess. I know I'll have to buy a new door."

Danny looked down at the puddle of pee. "I gather Brimley's a problem?"

"My ex-husband dropped him off a month ago. Said he didn't want him, and he was my dog anyway. He howls when I'm gone and scratches the door. Sometimes he chews on the table legs."

"What does he do when you're home?"

"Oh, he stays right by me. He's quiet then, but when I pick up my tennis racket or get my jacket, he starts baying and barking."

"Separation anxiety," he said. "It's hard to fix. Sounds like Brimley's afraid to be alone."

"Can you do anything?"

"It'll take a while, and you have to be willing to stay with it. We have to work with toys, treats, and smells, and you should go to the vet and get some anti-anxiety medication like amitriptyline."

"Could you write that down?"

"Just tell the vet that Brimley has an anxiety problem and he howls and chews when you leave the house."

"Will you help with extra training?"

"Go to the vet and get a prescription. Then let me know, and we'll talk about it."

For the next week, Danny's mind wandered, and one night he awoke from a dream where Doris was running by him naked and in slow motion, waving. *Damn, here come the thoughts again. Need to get to a meeting.*

Danny had five years of sobriety except for one slip with marijuana over a year ago. No one would want to live that year again. His compassion for animals had led him into a legal fight with a powerful woman who ran a well-funded dog and cat shelter. He was laid off from his job with the animal shelter where he was working, and had to fight a libel and slander lawsuit. Ida almost lost her job over the whole thing, and his anxiety ramped up, keeping him off balance and barely able to cope. His mind filled with shotgun fantasies and anger; then he would swing to confusion, obsessive and endless plans, and when he was fatigued and lonely, his mind would fill with lust. His world became pornographic or at least photogenic, and his imagination ran wild.

When Ida was there, when he could see her, or even smell her, he more easily felt normal. The jasmine fragrance that surrounded her seemed to settle his anxiety, even better than the benzodiazepine prescription he carried but didn't like to use. In his normal state, his compassion took over, and he would become absorbed in pet therapy with Jedi at the hospitals, or teaching dog training classes. He still attended his AA meetings and stayed in touch with his sponsor, Mark. Two scars on his forehead from the fire were still streaked with deep red. Danny had always surrounded himself with animals. He had a way with them, and people who knew him well understood that Danny often listened and talked with dogs in ways they clearly understood. He could often see the confusion and fear in a dog's mind, and he had a calming presence.

Two weeks later, Dusty and Brimley returned to class. Brimley was drooling and seemed almost asleep. "Well, we're back," Dusty said.

Danny smiled. "Is Brimley okay? He looks drugged."

"I gave him an extra pill before class. That way he won't bother anyone."

"He's not going to learn much in this condition." Danny kneeled and held Brimley's head with both hands, looking into his dull eyes.

Once again, Dusty waited after class. "Well, I did what you said. Can you come over and help?"

Danny looked up at the buzzing florescent lights as a queasy feeling arose in his throat. He could use the extra money. He could teach her about dog toys, rawhide chews, leaving dirty underwear on Brimley's bed, successive approximation to longer absent times—maybe it wouldn't be too bad. His mind wandered, and he could tell she needed someone. "I'll tell you what. I can come over ten times for twenty dollars an hour. If you stay with it, we can probably train Brimley to stop barking. I can't make any guarantees, though."

"I've got to try. His howling is going to get me run out of my apartment."

Danny met her at five pm on Friday evenings and worked with Brimley for an hour. When Danny arrived, Brimley wagged his tail and settled right down. Danny regulated Brimley's medication, manipulated the environment, and taught Dusty to leave for a few minutes, then 10 minutes, then 20 minutes, and then an hour. She kept her tennis racket in her car, along with her jacket and other signs of her absence. She was a little squeamish about handing Danny dirty underwear, but he quickly arranged them in a circle around Brimley's soft foam bed. She took Brimley to a dog camp during the week, picked him up at the same time every day, fed him with regularity, and increased his medication when he got jittery. After about six weeks, Brimley had settled down and seemed happy enough chewing a rawhide.

"Let me make dinner so we can celebrate," Dusty said. "That's the least I can do. You've done wonders with Brimley."

"We're not done yet. This will take months."

"How about some pasta and mushroom sauce? I've got salad too."

"Sure. I guess it would be okay for me to stay for a while."

He stayed late into the evening, he talking about his pet therapy and, like Brimley, his anxiety when alone; she talking about her ex-husband, her tennis playing, and her need for a friend she could trust. Danny stood up abruptly, thinking of Ida. He smiled. "Thanks for dinner. I've got to go now."

Dusty walked him to the door, touched his shoulder, turning him toward her, offering her lips. She stood two inches taller than he did, and she seemed eager, almost commanding. "You could stay a little longer, I mean, if you want to."

This was it. This was the crossing-over place. Dusty stood there with a warm invitation glowing at him from all over her body. He was lonely. Ida didn't understand. She was on a wild goose chase. He was holding down the home front, trying to keep it together, a good man in a slippery place.

"Better go," Danny said. "See you at class."

He yielded to her next invitation for dinner and stayed late into the night talking. He was appropriate, thoughtful, and even talked about Ida and their plans for a wedding in August.

"Where is she?"

"She's somewhere in Canada searching for a half brother. She thinks her mother had a baby boy that no one ever knew about."

Dusty put her hand on his arm. "I'm not interested in anything serious. I'm just lonely. Maybe we're like two people passing in the night who stopped to give each other a little comfort."

That was enough. Danny crossed over, but as Dusty unbuttoned her blouse, revealing no bra, he looked over at Brimley thumping his tail on the floor, head cocked and tongue hanging out. Danny shook his head. "You're beautiful, Dusty, but something tells me this is not a good idea."

"What's the matter?" she asked as he drew away. "I can see what you need."

"I guess it's pretty clear, all right, but I'm not going to feel right about it tomorrow."

She hugged him, pulling him to her, tight, with both arms. "All right then."

On the night of his last visit, Dusty had prepared beef stroganoff, fresh vegetables, and a salad. She lit candles, the flickering light making shadows on her lean, tan arm. Brimley slept quietly on his bed, his nose poked into rumpled white panties. She smiled at Danny through eyelashes with fresh mascara. "You've become important around here," she said.

Danny ate quietly, feeling unbalanced, as though he was in strange territory. Ida was in the back of his mind, and as he swallowed bites of food, he felt stuffy, and the food went down too slowly. The sauce from the stroganoff seemed to stick in his throat.

Later, with his shirt off, in her bed between flowered sheets, he squeezed his eyes shut and buried his face in the nape of her neck, but try as he might, he could not make her feel or smell like Ida. Instead of warm and soft, Dusty felt cool and rubbery, as though her skin might squeak at his touch. Danny was too troubled to perform. She reached down to unbutton his jeans and to touch him there, but he groaned halfheartedly and rolled over on his side. *Well, that's enough of that.* He got up, put on his shirt, and walked to the door. Dusty followed, a sheet wrapped around her. Danny turned toward her. "I think Brimley will be okay now. Thank you for dinner. I should go home."

"I guess you're right—we've passed in the night, just not as close as I would have liked. I guess we'll just go on."

Danny leaned down and scratched Brimley's ear. He put one paw on Danny's foot and whined. "You'll be okay, Brimley. Be nice to Dusty."

6

*I*da and Beth arrived at Port Sidney marina about two pm, walked quickly to the D dock, and turned toward D-20. Dorothy and Paul McHugh were sitting on the back deck having a glass of wine. Dorothy stood up and waved. "We've been waiting. Would you like some tea?"

"Sure," Ida said. They stepped onto the back of *Destiny*, and then inside to the counter and sat on stools. Dorothy put cups in front of them. "Drink your tea and then we'll walk around and meet some folks."

Paul leaned on his crutch, grinning. "It's nice to meet some new people," he said. "This boating life can get lonely sometimes." Dorothy frowned, turning to Ida. "Come on, let's get going."

They walked down the E dock, greeting friends and asking questions. Paul clomped along behind on his crutch. Then they walked down the F dock and out to the Custom's Dock, where two officers were busy checking a large yacht from Seattle. One officer nodded and said hello, trying to maintain an official stance as he stared, open-mouthed, at Ida. He grinned, raised one eyebrow, and glanced just past Ida at Beth standing behind her. Ida smiled, dropping her eyes. "Can I ask you a question?"

"Yes, ma'am."

"Do you ever see research boats from Vancouver?"

He shuffled his feet. "Now and then."

"I'm looking for a professor who is on a research project for the summer—name's Joel Martin, and he's a marine biologist—specializes in killer whales."

"Can't say as I've heard of him, but if he's doing research for the summer, my guess is that he's up north, somewhere around the Orca Lab in Johnstone Strait—the lab's on Hanson Island. Best place to check is Alert Bay, someone there probably knows."

"How far is that?"

"You could call the harbormaster at the marina up there—it's about 425 kilometers, ah, 265 miles by boat, or you can drive."

Ida looked at the officer's badge, Greg Bartley. "Officer Bartley, would it be all right with you if I said you suggested I call? It might help."

He took a rumpled card from his pocket and handed it to Ida. "Sure, use my card. I know most of the harbormasters on the island. We have a good network."

Ida led the way back to *Destiny*, and Dorothy found a travel book with all the marinas listed. She found the phone number for Alert Bay. "Here, use my cell phone. Yours will cost a fortune." It rang seven times before someone answered. "Chris Klinger here, Harbormaster."

Ida explained, using Officer Bartley's name, and there was a long pause. "You know, there are several boats around here doing research, but I don't know the name Joel Martin. You might check out at the Orca Labs— here, let me give you the number."

No one answered at Orca Labs, so Ida left a message.

"Please stay for dinner," Dorothy said. "Paul can fire up the grill for hamburgers, and I've got salad and ice cream."

Beth glanced at Ida. She nodded. "That would be great. We can wait for a return call."

Paul drank and cooked, leaning on his crutch, and Dorothy set the table, and then she, Ida, and Beth climbed the stairs to the flybridge, and arranged chairs so they could sit and watch the sunset. "This is beautiful," Dorothy said, "but sitting in this marina is getting on my nerves. Paul drinks more when there's nothing to do, and he's taking too many pain pills."

Ida leaned in close, talking in a quiet voice. "When do you think he'll be up for traveling?"

"We could probably leave when he gets his new walking cast, about two weeks, but I'm worried he can't handle the boat. He's sure he can, but I don't know."

"You're quite fit," Beth said. "I'll bet you could almost handle the boat by yourself."

"It's not that easy. This trawler is bigger than you think, and the wind can push you around, especially in the marinas."

Her phone rang. "Oh, yes, just a minute." She handed the phone to Ida. "It's someone from Orca Labs."

Ida took the phone. "Hello. Thank you for calling...I see, thank you." She smiled at Beth. "A boat called *Spyhopper* has been around the area, and there's a man named Troy who lives on the boat. They said a professor named Martin came up in June with some people from the University. He's there, up by Alert Bay somewhere, about 260 miles north."

"How far is it by water?" Dorothy asked.

"Depends on the stops, but about the same, counting in and out of harbors. If you figure eighty kilometers a day, and that's pushing it, say five or six days. I'd figure a week in case of weather."

Dorothy pasted on an impish smile, stood up, and crossed her arms. "How would you girls like to crew—you know, help us with the boat? We are going around the island, and we could leave now with some help."

Ida raised her eyebrows. "What would we do to help?"

"Cook, clean, help with docking, drive some—things like that. One of you could take that little bedroom, and the couch makes into a nice bed. We'd stay at marinas. It would be safe. We could drop you off in Alert Bay."

Beth took Ida by the crook of her arm. "I'm tired of working on that whale-watching boat. I'd have to call them, but I'm up for a little adventure."

"I've come this far, and I want to find Joel Martin. What do we do next?"

Dorothy turned to Paul. He opened a bottle of wine and poured himself a glass. "I'm ready to go. I don't need the help, but we could use the company."

"Can you girls be back here in the morning? We should take a day and practice with the boat, and we'll need more provisions."

Ida turned to Beth, and they both shook their heads in unison. "We'll close up my place and be back here about noon," Beth said.

Paul grinned. "It's about time we got going."

"We'll go over things on the boat tomorrow, and then we can spend Tuesday out in the bay. We'll go to Telegraph Harbor on Wednesday, and stay the night there."

"I've got the whole trip around the island planned out," Paul said. He opened a travel book and pointed at the route drawn with a yellow marker.

"See. Here's Telegraph Harbor on Thetis Island or, if the weather's nice, we can go on to Silva Bay the first night—about eighty kilometers."

Ida took Dorothy's hand. "Are you sure about this? I don't know anything about boats."

Dorothy lowered her voice and pointed at Paul. "It will be a relief. I need some other people around so I don't beat him to death."

Ida forced a laugh as she and Beth hurried to the car.

"I've been waiting for something like this," Beth said. "My life has been pretty dull." They drove to the motor home, each lost in their own thoughts.

Beth pulled up and parked. "This sounds selfish," she said, "but could you give me a couple of hours alone? I need to make some calls and send some emails. You're welcome to take the car."

"Sure, let me get a jacket, and I'll take a walk. It's a beautiful afternoon."

Ida walked along the shore for a mile before calling Danny. Now he would have to believe her. People had heard of Joel Martin, and she knew she could find him. A research project would take time, so he wouldn't be wandering all over the place. In a week she would be there. She sat down on a rock and dialed.

"Ida—are you doing okay? Where are you?"

"I'm still at Beth's, but I found Joel Martin. I mean I found out where he is—north about two hundred and sixty miles."

"Where's that?"

"Have you got the map of Vancouver Island?"

"Right here by the phone."

"He's near Telegraph Cove and Alert Bay. They say he's on a boat doing research on killer whales. I'm sure I can track him down."

"Then what?"

"Then I'll find out, that's what."

"Sorry, I mean if he's your half brother, then what's next?"

"We'll just have to go from there—it depends on how he reacts."

"What do you think, maybe a week or so?"

"Guess what, Beth and I are going to help this older couple with their new boat. We're going up the Inside Passage to Cormorant Island—Alert Bay. It'll take about a week, and they'll let us off there. There's seaplane service back to Victoria. I'd say two weeks."

"There's no telling what his reaction will be. What if he doesn't want to be found?"

"I guess we'll find out. I'm not giving up now."

"No, I'm sure you won't. Stay in touch."

"How are the dogs?"

"They miss you, but I let both of them sleep on the bed—in your place. They don't smell as good, though."

Ida sighed and raised her eyes to a billowy cloud that floated in the sky. It seemed shaped like a killer whale. "I guess you'll do what you want with those dogs. I miss them, too, and you. Bye for now."

Ida zipped up her blue fleece as the breeze came up and made ripples on the water. She crossed her arms, put her head down, and walked into the breeze. She checked her watch, and it had been over two hours. As she walked up the bank trail, she saw a Canadian Customs SUV beside Beth's motor home. She approached slowly, and from about 20 yards away, she could hear the gasps and moans—sex sounds? Ida stood quietly until the sounds quieted and then walked up to the door and opened it. "Beth, it's Ida, I'm back."

She heard some rustling and then saw Greg Bartley come out of the bedroom hitching up his service belt and arranging his flashlight, Mace, and handcuffs. Ida raised one eyebrow slightly and put her hands on her hips. "Hello, Mr. Bartley."

His skin turned bright pink. "Oh, hello. Nice to see you again."

Beth came out behind him pulling a white terrycloth robe together, her face relaxed and bright. "Greg came by to visit," she said.

Greg turned sideways, eyes ignoring Ida, and jumped into his SUV, his athletic shoulders leading the way. His lack of interest in her body befuddled Ida. Hadn't they connected at the dock? She had seen his desire. Ida crossed her arms and chewed her lip. What happened to her power, the dependable power she gathered from men's desires? For more than twenty years, she had cultivated the art of how she was seen—the hitch of her bra, the gentle sway of her hips, her innocent blank stare through glistening eyes, touching men's chests, and a face full of earnest attention. These had been calculated acts of will after her teenage experiences in youth group, but soon became thoughtless habits of countenance, permanent lures trolling through the waters of her life. She had come to believe a man's desire was a spiritual force she could control and use, and normally it was. What was with Greg Bartley?

She turned to Beth and noticed, for the first time, how shapely and young she seemed, her smile revealing a naturally sensual woman. Maybe he was drawn to her because she's a social worker—likes to help people and make them feel good. By the looks of things, she sure helped Greg.

"Do you know him from somewhere?" Ida asked.

"Yes, years ago I worked with his family to get them some assistance. He was a teenager then, but I've always thought he was gorgeous. Had no idea we'd ever meet again."

"He's got to be twenty years younger than you."

"Twenty-one years, I think. He just turned thirty-two, and I was fifty-four in April. Yes, so that would be twenty-one years—he's smokin' handsome, don't you think?" She crossed her arms and hugged her breasts, twisting side to side. "I need to thank you."

Ida frowned. "For what?"

"If I hadn't met you, I'd still be on the whale-watching boat. It's been a long time, Ida, a long time. I've almost forgotten what it's like to be ravished."

Ravished? That would mean surrender, not her style. She enjoyed sex, but there was an ebb and flow of desire, always to her liking—and she could simply not live unless she was wanted. When she gave a man pleasure, she extinguished his flame like the flood tide becoming slack, and then as the waves receded, she would again set her sails to catch the winds of desire. Deep down, she believed she could navigate her days with male yearning, a magical compass that guided her life. But Greg? Not even a glance.

7

*I*da and Beth handed their bags over the back rail to Dorothy as Paul appeared with a cart full of groceries and wine. Everything was moved onto the back deck, and Dorothy began sorting through bags and putting things away in the galley. "You should take the bedroom," she said to Beth. "Just put your bags in there on the bed. Ida, you can have the couch. It slides out into a very comfortable bed." Paul opened the hatch to the engine room and checked all the fluid levels, and then made his way up six steps to the bridge and made some entries in the log book. He looked down the stairs. "Hey, everyone, today will be a practice day. We'll run out by Moresby Island, check over the boat, practice driving, and come back in time for dinner. Maybe twenty kilometers altogether. I figure three or four hours." He started the engine and came down the stairs and motioned to Ida and Beth. They followed him out the door onto the back deck as he explained how to disconnect the power cord. Ida and Beth stepped back onto the dock, unplugged the cord, rolled it up, and handed it over the rail to Dorothy. He handed them a bright orange cone to mark their dock space as occupied. Then everyone made their way along the side up onto the bow as Dorothy showed Ida and Beth the bow line and a locker where the fenders were stored when they were underway. "I'll show you, but the idea is to untie the bow line and hook it on the cleat. Then, you just flip the line loose when Paul says we're ready to cast off. Same thing on the stern line." Dorothy showed them how to pull up the fenders, unhook them, and stow them away in the locker. "Come on," she said, "let's go up top on the flybridge. That's the best place to drive when we're around the docks. You can see everything, and the controls are easy."

They gathered at the wheel as Paul showed them the controls—forward, reverse, neutral, and engine speed. He put Ida's hand on a small joy stick. "Okay, now watch this." He moved the joystick to the right, and the bow pulled tight against the line. "This is the bow thruster. It moves the bow left or right, and this one is the stern thruster. Does the same for the back of the boat."

They cast off without incident, and Paul drove slowly out the waterway between D and E docks. They had to wait for several boats to move out of the way near the customs dock, and then turned into the entrance channel. "Have to stay right in the center, in the deepest part." He cursed under his breath as a large sailboat came in. He had to move close to the rocks as they eased by each other. "Damn sailboats. We get a little wind, and they come and go all day. Too much work for me."

Paul took them out about five kilometers near Moresby and idled. Ida and Beth each practiced driving from the flybridge and from inside. They practiced turns, backing up, turning with the bow thruster and stern thruster, coiling lines, throwing the man-overboard ring, and fitting their inflatable life jackets. Dorothy showed them the fire extinguishers, the first aid kits, and how to pump out the sewage holding tank.

Paul keyed up the radio microphone. "This is *Destiny*, *Destiny*, *Destiny*. South of Moresby Island. Can I have a radio check please?" They heard a crackle. "*Destiny*, this is *Windy Day*. You are loud and clear. *Windy Day* out."

"We'll practice on the radio after we get going tomorrow," Paul said. The wind had come up quickly from a silver-blue sky, and some billowy clouds formed on the eastern horizon near Vancouver. "Going to get blustery. We should head back to the marina."

Beth pulled her hat down to shade her eyes and pointed. "Look, out there, killer whales."

The whales were about 100 meters off the starboard bow moving with the speed of the boat. Ida rushed up the stairs to the flybridge as Beth followed and handed her the binoculars.

"I think it's them," Ida said. "Mike, Slick, and Alki. Do you think they know we're on this boat?"

"They're coming this way."

"Those whales chase off all the salmon," Paul said. "The fishing has been ruined around here."

Dorothy crossed her arms and frowned. "I think it's more about the ferries, water taxis, and all the chemicals from the refining companies—those are the problems. The salmon are dying off because the whole place is getting polluted."

Paul waved a hand at her in disgust. "Dorothy has become an expert tree hugger in her old age."

The whales disappeared for a couple of minutes and then surfaced 50 meters behind them. Ida ran down the stairs to the back deck, leaned against the rail, and waved her arms over her head. The whales dove again, then, just 25 meters out, Mike surged up spyhopping. In the flash of the sun on a whitecapped wave, they disappeared. Had Mike seen her? Did he know she was on the way north?

Paul turned into the entranceway to the marina, turned right after E dock, and drove slowly into the wind down the waterway. "Sonofabitch," he said. "A damn sailboat has taken our slip. Dorothy, did you put out the orange cone?"

"Of course we did. They just ignored it."

The brisk wind was blowing toward the sailboat and directly at the bow of *Destiny*. Paul held *Destiny* still and called the harbormaster. "This is *Destiny*...there's a sailboat in our slip. We left the cone out."

"Sorry about that. Just take the next slip. I'll send down some deck-hands to help—bow in and tie up your starboard side."

Paul cursed and straightened up his crutch. The wind was blowing directly at the bow at about 10 knots. This would be tricky. Dorothy stood beside him. "Go ahead past the dock and then turn. The wind will catch you right away, so steer clear of the sailboat." Paul pushes her with his hip. "Get out of my way. I need to concentrate."

He turned sharply, added power—too much—whacked into the dock, and then the stern bounced against an orange ball suspended on the portside bow of the sailboat. Paul turned white, gritted his teeth, quickly jammed into reverse, and leaned full on the stern thruster. He barely cleared the sailboat as he backed into the waterway. The wind caught the bow, and the boat turned. Paul leaned too quickly on his crutch, and he fell. Dorothy grabbed the wheel, reduced power, and drove slowly down the waterway. As Paul stood up, he saw dozens of people come out of their boats to watch him.

"*Destiny*, this is the harbormaster. Go down to the end, turn around, and come back slowly. Watch for the deckhand at the end of the dock. He will guide you."

Dorothy scampered down the stairs and reminded Beth and Ida to wait and toss their coiled lines when a deckhand signaled. Beth was on the bow, and Ida was at the stern, coiled lines in hand. Dorothy checked the fenders on the starboard side and then dropped three fenders down on the port side in case they hit the sailboat. After Paul had turned around and headed back down the waterway, they noticed the crowd had grown. It was cocktail time, and people waved their drinks. Men shouted advice. "Slow down, mate; speed up; watch your stern; turn quickly." Three men on the sailboat had dropped two more orange balls, and they stood like sentries waiting for an assault. Three deckhands in blue Port Sidney polo shirts stood along the dock. The deckhand on the end motioned to Paul and began to direct him like the ground crew at the airport. Paul turned, backed up a little, then aimed straight into the slip and powered ahead, using the bow and stern thrusters to steer. His speed was a little too fast, and the deckhand motioned for reverse just as Beth threw a line into a man's waiting hands. He wrapped it around the upright, trying to pull *Destiny* toward the dock. Paul felt the pull and pushed the wrong way on the stern thruster, and the port stern bounced off two orange balls on the bow of the sailboat. A man on the sailboat tried to push *Destiny* with a pole, but the wind was too strong. Paul pushed full bore on the stern thruster, started to come around, and a deckhand motioned to Ida to toss him the line. Dorothy yelled at Paul, "Reverse, you idiot, but just a touch." *Destiny* moved suddenly backward just as Ida threw the line, slipped on the deck, and caught her fall on the rail. She watched the line uncoil in the air, as if in slow motion, and then drop into the water, disappearing under the boat. A deckhand jumped onto the stern swim step holding another line, tied it to a stern cleat, and tossed the line to another deckhand just as Dorothy shouted, "Neutral, idiot, neutral," and Ida's sinking line got sucked into the prop.

"Power off," shouted one deckhand as the three of them pulled *Destiny* against the dock and then forward. Paul threw his crutch down the stairs and came down holding the rails. He shouted at Ida. "Don't you know anything? You almost broke the prop."

Dorothy scampered down the stairs. "You're the one who caused it."

Paul turned to Dorothy, shaking his fist in her face. "You always screw things up. I knew what I was doing."

Beth walked in between them and took Dorothy's hand. "It's over now. Let's get some tea."

The three men on the sailboat shook their heads as Ida held out her upturned palms and shrugged. "No problem," one man said, grinning. Suddenly Ida felt the breeze on her breast. Her spaghetti strap pink top had come down when she threw the line, and she was hanging out on her right side. She turned and fixed her strap, pulling herself back together. Another man shouted, "You can bump into us anytime."

Ida moved toward Paul. "Sorry about the rope, but the boat backed up fast."

"It's a line, Ida, not a rope."

"Okay, sorry about the line. I thought it was longer."

Paul scrambled off the boat with his crutch, fished five dollars out of his pocket, and gave it to a deckhand, shaking his head. "Women. Hey mate, can you help my wife hook up the power?"

He took off down the dock, crutch slung over his shoulder, limping on his boot.

Beth helped Dorothy uncoil the yellow electric cord as she handed the male end to the deckhand, along with ten dollars. "This is for your friends. You guys saved us from a real disaster."

"Where's Paul going?" Beth asked.

"To the washroom and then the bar. We won't see him again until after dark. Why don't you girls walk to the restaurant for some fish and chips. I don't feel like cooking."

Ida nodded, slipped on a blue rain jacket over her maroon sweats, and walked up the dock with Beth. A light mist floated in the air as the dock lights came on. She looked over her shoulder and noticed the three men on the sailboat watching her walk. Never mind Greg Bartley. She still turned men's heads. She added a little sashay to her next step, like the flip of a fishtail.

Ida and Beth sat by the window at the Captain's Table and each ordered a pint while they looked over the menu. "I don't know why I look at the menu," Beth said. "The best thing to get is always fish and chips."

Ida looked up as two of the men from the sailboat came in, recognizing them. Robert, the tall one, smiled. "Okay if we join you?"

Beth looked at Ida and shrugged her shoulders, motioning to a chair. Robert sat down next to Ida. "I'm Robert, and this here is my friend Pierre."

They both ordered pints. Robert leaned close to Ida. "You're from the US, right?"

"Yes, from Albuquerque."

"That's a long way—New Mexico, right?"

"Yes, about a half-million people, right in the middle of the state."

"I hail from up north, Powell River. Been a fisherman most of my life. Pierre here talked me into a sailing trip, but I'm partial to power boats."

Ida looked at his large hands. They were calloused and cracked, the hands of a working man. Long, tousled, light brown hair fell along the sides of his angular face, and his sparkling blue eyes topped a broad smile and a ruddy nose. He looked to be about 10 years older than Ida. She noticed he didn't wear a wedding ring about the same time that he glanced at her left hand. Somehow, from a place Ida didn't understand, a gentle warmth spread over her body, as if his hopeful desire had become a soft cloud, a puff of breeze, and a touch of silk, together making her skin tingle. She touched her neck. She gazed over Robert's head and imagined Danny's smile and their kitchen, her dog ER hopping into her lap, and the comfort of her own bed. Yet there he was, blue eyes ranging over her, searching for another hint, perhaps a deep breath highlighting her breasts, or a touch on the back of his hand. His yearning came from deep in his eyes. Her power amped up as he shifted in his seat. "Are you married?"

"No. I am engaged, and we plan to be married in August."

"Sorry, I didn't see a ring."

Ida smiled. "I'm a critical care nurse, and jewelry tears my gloves."

"Are you on a holiday?"

"No, I'm looking for someone, a family member. Beth and I hitched a ride with Paul and Dorothy—the owners of *Destiny*, the boat next to your sailboat. They are traveling around Vancouver Island."

"New boat, new captain, right?" Robert smiled.

"Yes. Beth and I are having second thoughts, but the boat's easy to drive, and it'll only be a few days. They'll drop us off at Alert Bay. I think he's on a killer whale research boat somewhere in the area."

After dinner and a few more pints, Robert stood up, taking Ida's hand. "Can I walk you home?" His smile seemed even warmer, and Ida's eyes met his. She let him pull her hand gently as she stood up, scooting her chair back, shaking her hair. A gentle magnetism arose between them, and Ida's neck warmed. Robert licked his lips and then wiped his mouth with a napkin. "Good food, good brew, beautiful woman—can't ask for more than that."

Ida walked with her chin up and her chest high, holding his hand, feeling strong beside this man who admired her so. He stopped at the rear deck of *Destiny*, and then raised her hand toward the sailboat. "Want to see our boat?"

"I guess. I've never been on a sailboat."

"Come on then."

He helped her up on the deck and then opened the door to below. "Beautiful woodwork, nice galley, and plenty of sleeping room."

Ida stepped down, slipped off her rain jacket, and backed up next to the galley sink. "My gosh, I didn't realize how much room there is."

He motioned forward. "Full head with a shower." He moved close to Ida and touched the side of her cheek. "You have beautiful hair."

"Thank you," she said, kissing him quickly on the cheek. "You're a nice man."

He moved closer, leaned down, and kissed her lips gently. Ida put her arms around his neck and they kissed again, her tongue flicked his once, then withdrew. Her heart pounded, trapped in a shadowy place where his desire radiated, warming her thighs, but for some reason made a cold shiver run up her back. Without warning, he reached around, put his hands down the inside of her sweatpants, and squeezed her cheeks. Ida quickly tightened; because his rough, scarred hands suddenly did not feel like desire, because he was suddenly lifting Ida off her feet and pressing her against him with incredible strength, and because his thick, damp lips tasted fishy, she pushed herself away with an awkward burst of strength. "I've got to go now." She turned her head as Robert pulled his hands out of her pants. "What's the matter? You were coming on to me just fine up at the restaurant."

"Sorry, don't mean to be a tease, but this doesn't feel right."

Ida scooped up her rain jacket, scrambled up the steps and out on the deck. Robert followed. "Maybe another time," he said, pinching her bottom.

Ida hopped off the boat, took five big steps, and then jumped onto the back of *Destiny*. Dorothy greeted her at the door. "Oh, you're back. Everything okay with you?"

"Yes. How about a cup of tea?"

"You're shaking. You should be wearing your jacket."

"You're right. Shouldn't have taken it off."

8

On the northern reach of Johnstone Strait, near Cormorant Island and Alert Bay, Professor Joel Martin sat in his captain's seat at the helm of the killer whale research boat *Spyhopper*, a converted 62-foot old wood seiner. He was positioning the vessel for anchorage in a quiet cove in the Parsons Islands, just past Telegraph Cove, about three km from Blackney Pass, near the known pathways of over 180 northern resident killer whales, and near the Orca Lab research station on the southeast shore of Hanson Island. Troy Campbell, Joel's longtime friend and first mate of *Spyhopper*, had unhooked the anchor chain and was motioning to come ahead. "Come ahead about ten meters," he shouted from the bow.

Troy's light brown ponytail hung out from under a floppy, khaki rain hat, and his black tank-top shirt revealed his lean arms and body, as well as the fading tattoos of Orcas and dolphins on his upper arms. Joel leaned his head out the window, checking behind him. He touched the throttle. "Wind will bring us there now." Joel had purchased *Spyhopper* in disrepair three years ago, and Troy had lived aboard for the past two years, restoring the old vessel to workable condition. Troy was a quiet, withdrawn man—a loner—and maintained his peace of mind by listening to eagles, ravens, and killer whales; he kept his hands busy with projects.

Hazel Chartrand, a marine biology graduate student, stood next to Troy, looking into the water for unexpected rocks. A striking woman with black hair, a round face, and thick, strong thighs, she had earned the job of research assistant by her good grades and her familiarity with the area.

"Starboard side is clear," said Hazel, smiling at Troy. She was a quiet 32-year-old, wore her jet-black hair tied back, and moved with a settled balance, as though she was comfortable on solid ground and aboard a rocking boat. She had been born nearby on Cormorant Island, her father a Russian fisherman, and her mother a Kwakiutl Indian from Malcolm Island. Sturdy, warm, and gentle, Hazel had a mysterious smile and bright dark eyes, as though she carried secrets from the past. Her senses were keen and gave the impression that she was matter-of-fact about her desires. She lifted her chin and leaned back slightly when standing, as though she was ready and waiting for whatever the world might bring. Her wide hips, cinnamon breath, ample bosom, and quiet manner often made men open up and share private thoughts and dreams, wishing, perhaps, they could lie back and rest in the comfort of her lap. As a young woman, she left the island for college and became a paralegal in Vancouver. In the summer of 2002, she decided to return to graduate school in anthropology and marine biology, a combination that would help her preserve the culture and heritage of her ancestors. Hazel often spoke of bears, ravens, eagles, and Orcas, revealing her belief in her kinship with all living things, and her graduate studies focused on killer whales and their role in Kwakiutl culture. Hazel wore jersey tops, no bra, running shorts, and old, rugged tennis shoes. Sweats and raincoats were hung around the boat for when the sun could not shine through the weather.

Jean climbed the five stairs up to the wheelhouse. "This is not a good place to anchor. There's land on three sides. We can't hear anything from here."

"I've been on the radio," Joel said. "The reception is fine. There's a storm coming from the southeast, and we need to be tucked in. There's wind and a two-meter flood tide in the morning. We can swing on the anchor in here without hitting any rocks."

"That's what I love about you. You're always thinking ahead, and you're always right—except for the times when I am." She forced a little smile.

"Well, that's not this time. What are you thinking about for dinner?"

"I've got a big pot of fish stew on the stove. It's halibut with new potatoes, carrots, pearl onions, and leeks."

Joel motioned to Troy to release the anchor, and the chain rattled over the pulley. "That sounds great. I'm starving." The chain went slack at about 20 meters. "We've got plenty of water." He motioned to Troy to set the chain. Joel backed up *Spyhopper* a couple of meters until the anchor caught.

"Let's all have dinner together," Joel said. "I want to go over this project again and again until everyone is tuned into the same space and time. We might only hear this particular dialect for a few minutes, and I want to be sure we get it."

"Sure, I'll finish up and let the girls know. Should be about an hour."

Jean Jeffry, a marine biology professor and Joel's research partner, often sat in the galley at the table, sulking and biting her lip with yellowed teeth from years of smoking, a habit she had quit at the beginning of the summer. She was 50 and had been a university teacher for 20 years. Even when seated, Jean's long neck made her appear tall, and her pursed lips, high cheekbones, and furrowed brow created an air of superiority. Her countenance made her appear to be thinking all the time, like Joel, and observing the world earnestly and endlessly for breakthrough ideas on killer whales and eagle behavior. She seemed too lean, and gave the impression that her nervous energy absorbed her meals before the calories could spread through her body. Sometimes a thought arose in her mind that, with the exception of her mentor Joel, too many stupid people surrounded her, and they somehow had formed a conspiracy to make her unhappy, which, of course, they did. She believed that when she and Joel could one day consummate their love with waves of passion, then she would have an ally, and together they would be stronger than any conspiracy could muster, and newfound happiness and academic notoriety would soon follow. Joel and Jean had remained strictly professional in public, but frolicked like rabbits in private.

Jean did most of the cooking, so the galley was her domain. At this moment, Jean was sure this was not the correct place to anchor. And, even though the sun was bright, Hazel should be wearing more clothes. A gray jersey sports bra and running shorts were not appropriate, especially without underwear. Joel had been getting an eyeful since the trip began, and Jean didn't like feeling nauseated when Joel smiled at Hazel. Ever since she and Joel started sleeping together at UBC five years ago, Jean had envisioned a closer, public relationship. Because they were both faculty; because he needed her scientific credibility to get his grants to study Orcas;

and because, she thought, he was sometimes embarrassed to be affection-
ate in public, Joel had insisted on keeping their relationship private. On
campus, he called her Dr. Jeffry and insisted she call him Dr. Martin. Yet,
with both of them single and growing older, Joel in his late 40s and Jean
having turned 50 in April, isolated on a boat together for the summer, she
knew she could bring the intimacy to Joel he must surely be craving, and he
would soon announce their engagement—it was time they were more than
sex partners, enjoyable as it was. They were both incredibly smart, and they
shared the dream of being leaders in Orca research. Why not a married
couple? There were other husband-wife teams at UBC.

Joel slept in a small captain's cabin underneath the pilothouse. Troy
stayed by himself in the crew sleeping area down below in the fo'c'sle, at-
tending the contrary diesel engine. He read all the time, avoided contact or
conversation, and he was generally not available to people, although when
his attention was sought, he presented a smile underneath a crooked nose
and warm brown eyes. He kept his head down when he walked and yet
seemed remarkably attuned to natural sounds, weather, and smells, especially any indicators of wildlife nearby. He always heard the killer whales
before others, and he could smell a diesel-powered fishing boat from two
kilometers away.

Hazel had a cabin on the port side of the stern, Jean stayed alone
in an adjacent cabin on the starboard side, and they shared a head and
shower—a consequence of the close quarters on the boat—four people in
1,000 square feet—that was particularly unpleasant for Jean. After Hazel
came out of the head, Jean would reach in, spray air freshener, and run the
fan for a few minutes before she sniffed and stepped in for her bathroom
activities. The smell of dirty clothes bothered her as well, so she fashioned
a large, sealing plastic hamper for Troy and Hazel to use until they could
get to Alert Bay and a Laundromat. Joel's smell didn't bother her. In fact,
the salty breeze made him smell fresh, like spruce trees. Jean did her best
to keep her kitchen clean, but the smell of burnt coffee, leaking whiffs of
smoke from the diesel stove, and leftover fish in the small refrigerator kept
Jean's nose wrinkled, often giving her face the look of an unhappy judge.

Joel and Troy shared the forward head and shower, and both women
blanched if they had to use the men's room. Both toilets required pumping

up seawater for a flush. The pipes, gaskets, and fittings had seen better days, so the mix of human smells was present no matter how much of Joel's homemade deodorant he flushed into the holding tank. His mix of borax, Pine Sol, and ammonia saved money, but left an acrid after-smell, like the puff of air that escapes when a plastic bag of dirty cat litter is tied shut.

Though only six feet tall, Joel commanded more than his share of attention. His wavy snow-white hair was full, and swept back loosely over his ears. His slender, moody, tight-lipped face would intermittently form a radiant smile with perfectly straight teeth, like a model for an orthodontist office. His smile, though captivating, was always a little too late for the moment, giving the impression that he may be a little daft, but he was actually quite brilliant and showed his intelligence with his thoughtful choice of words and his knowledge about killer whales, dolphins, and the biological sciences.

Jean was grateful that Joel would be present for dinner—fully present—not in a psychedelic trance, unreachable and finely tuned to the underwater sounds coming through those infernal earphones. She first saw him in a trance more than 20 years ago at a protest rally at the Vancouver Aquarium in 1984. She was completing her graduate work in marine biology and ornithology, and Joel had already published articles on *Orcinus orca* in a journal on cetaceans. He was fascinated with the work of John Lilly on dolphins, and he had marshaled a group of students to protest the captivity of killer whales, and specifically Bjossa, a female killer whale imprisoned at the aquarium, a protest that almost got him kicked out of graduate school.

Jean loved him at first sight when she met him in the parking lot that day, and she had managed, sometimes with months of interruption, to live in his vicinity and in her fantasy that they would someday become husband and wife. Five years ago, after a faculty party, Joel gave her a ride home and came in for a drink. Lonely and a little drunk, they fell into her bed. After that night, she knew, married or not, they would mate for life and soar into the future, like the bald eagles that nested, roamed, hunted, and played along the coastlines. Her deep love would lure him away from his work on interspecies communication long enough for him to discover the excitement of life-long companionship. Her yearning to be married sometimes filled her with waves of anguish, but his lips on her neck and her heels gripping his back chased the feelings away. An earnest woman, Jean had the capacity to love deeply, to maintain scientific objectivity in her work, to serve the crew healthy food, and to patiently wait for the moment he would propose marriage.

She remembered when Joel dropped LSD and stared into the Vancouver aquarium for hours on end, his eyes changing from green to gray and then back to green again. One of his scientific articles later claimed intimate, sensual, and prolonged mental contact with Bjossa. He wrote that every living thing has a spirit, deserves respect, and life forms can open the fabric of their spirits to interspecies communication. Often ridiculed by the scientific world, Joel focuses instead on the science of dialects—differences in their acoustic signals. Their particular squeals, whistles, squawks, and screams are unique to pods, and groups of pods, known as clans. The A, G, and R Clans do not have acoustic similarities with each other, and form the Northern Community, 16 pods in all. The J Clan, made up of three pods, is acoustically different from the other clans, and is known as the Southern Community. Joel believes there is a yet-undiscovered dialect, a particular sound, or song that can link the clans of the Northern Residents. That could lead to what he calls the Holy Grail, a sound that links the Northern Residents with the Southern Residents, and perhaps to the Transients, those killer whales that roam the open sea. The purpose of their research is to find that acoustic clue. His insistent claims gave him a shaky reputation as an objective scientist, but Jean's presence assured the grantors that any results would pass muster statistically and with repeatable results. Jean was his scientific backstop.

It troubled her that Joel has never been willing to talk about the year he took as sabbatical leave when Bjossa died at SeaWorld after having been moved from Vancouver, but she remembered that when he came back, his hair was white, and there was a permanent sadness that made deep wrinkles across his forehead. He had told her privately, however, that when he found the acoustic links, he would be able to show scientists the universal tie among all cetaceans, and then use that sound to recapture the blending of minds he had found with Bjossa. In academic circles, Jean had become known for her articles on births and the time calves spent with their mothers. She wrote that Orcas had signs and signals among themselves, squeaks and squawks that informed others of their mating status, and that available males traveled from other pods miles away. Jean Jeffry, PhD, was also the author of a small field guide about bald eagles, killer whales, and other mammals along the coastlines of Vancouver Island. She liked seeing "PhD" after her name and used it often. Joel preferred to avoid notoriety, likely because most people would not give credence to what he had learned from his psychedelic trances.

Jean banged a spoon on a dishpan. "Dinner is ready. Come on everyone."

The long table was open to the kitchen, and two sides were padded seats built against walls. There were portholes on both sides of the boat in the kitchen, and Jean had left them open to the breeze and salty pine smells that came in from the land and mixed with the steamy smell of fresh fish. The wind was gusting now, and *Spyhopper*'s round, wooden bottom was rocking in the growing waves. Troy sat at the end near Hazel, and Jean pulled up a stool to the other end of the table and began filling bowls with a ladle. Troy reached up and closed the porthole above him.

Jean put a plate on the table. "The bread is fresh out of the oven. Joel, will you please cut everyone a slice? Oh, the marmalade is strawberry, and save room for strawberry pie. I loaded up on fresh strawberries at our last grocery stop." Jean raised her chin, put her hands on her hips, and smiled as Joel nodded his approval. He raised his eyebrows slightly, his private signal that she should come to his cabin later. She nodded as he sliced bread for everyone. "You're a good cook and even a better research companion. I'm glad you're part of this trip." He smiled at Jean. "By the way, did you see those eagles swooping and diving? They put on quite a show."

Troy nodded. "I counted nine altogether, five yearlings."

"I got some good pictures," Jean said. "Now I can show my students that bald eagles know how to play catch." She grabbed her digital camera and showed everyone the viewer. "See, right there? They're playing catch with a herring. One eagle drops it, another catches it and takes it back up."

Troy cocked his head, a glint in his eyes. "That's an anchovy."

Jean frowned. "Close enough. The point is they're playing catch."

"I see that," Troy said.

Hazel smiled and put her hands together as though she was praying.

"My grandfather has seen them fall upside down holding a branch with their talons and then turn and swoop just before they hit the water. He told me he could hear the adult eagles laughing as they taught the yearlings. He said they know how to fly in the air and to glide in the spirit. Nice, don't you think? Fly in the air and glide in the spirit. I'll always remember that."

Joel moved his head up and down in agreement as he chewed on his fresh bread, strawberry marmalade oozing down his chin. Troy looked at his bowl as he ate quietly. Jean poured fresh coffee in Joel's cup, adding a little milk.

"That's a little esoteric for me," Jean said. "I suspect that your grandfather was influenced by Kwakiutl mythology, don't you?"

"When I was a little girl, he taught the children that the bald eagles bring power into the world from on high, and if we watch them carefully, we can learn how to survive most anything. I don't think that's mythology."

Under the table, Troy accidentally touched Hazel's knee, quickly moving his hand away.

"Have you started reading my field guide?"

"No, but it's next on my list."

"When you read it, I think you'll have a better understanding. I found a way of respecting the Kwakiutl culture and still staying with the scientific facts. I'll grant that bald eagles have keen senses, but I doubt that they carry power or glory or anything like that."

Hazel put a spoonful of stew in her mouth, swallowing quickly. "This is very good. Thank you for dinner."

Joel grabbed a fork, grinning. "I'm ready for that strawberry pie."

Jean put a plate in front of him, red strawberry juice oozing from the flaky crust. Jean knew her cooking was one way into Joel's heart. She also knew another way. That would come later.

9

*P*aul moved *Destiny* down the waterway, by the customs' dock, and out of the harbor. At six am the water was quiet, the sun was out, and there was no wind. It was a good day for travel. Paul sat on the flybridge in his heavy sweater. Dorothy brewed coffee in the galley; Ida and Beth sat up on the bow, faces turned to the rising sunshine. *Destiny* made her way northerly and then back to west. After about an hour, Paul cupped his hands and shouted. "Hey, Dorothy, come up here a minute." Dorothy climbed the stairs. "Just hold her steady at two hundred forty degrees. I want to move down into the pilothouse. I'll switch the controls from down there." Dorothy grabbed the wheel as Paul clumped down the steps.

Paul settled into the pilothouse, switched over the controls, and spread out his charts as Dorothy returned to the galley. Ida waved at Paul through the windshield. He nodded his head, but then focused on the chart. Dorothy brought him a cup of coffee and sat down beside him. "Show me where we are," she said, pointing to the chart.

"We've just rounded the top of the Saanich Peninsula, and we're in Satellite Channel. That's Swartz Bay back over there where the ferry docks."

Dorothy looked carefully. "You could've gone through here—John Passage—and saved going all the way around Coal Island. Would've saved a half hour."

"I didn't want to chance it. That seemed like a tight squeeze. Hey, give me a break. I've got to get used to the boat." He pushed on the throttle, increasing the speed to about 10 knots. *Destiny* settled down in the quiet water, cutting a smooth path easterly through Satellite Channel. Dorothy put her finger on the chart. "You're going through Sansum Narrows, right?"

"Yup. We should be able to see Maple Bay and then on up past Crofton to Chemainus, just like we said last night. I marked the whole way already. Can't you see the yellow marker?"

"Looks like Chemainus is about halfway."

"More or less. We should get to Gabriola Pass about four o'clock, and then into Silva Bay marina about five. It'll be a long day. We won't have time to dally, but I want to look at Pirate's Cove up here by Ruxton Passage." Paul reached into a cabinet under the chart table and took out a bottle of wine. Dorothy crossed her arms. "You won't get to see anything if you start this early." Paul ignored her and filled his empty coffee cup. "I need to stay relaxed. The captain's got a lot of responsibility, you know."

Dorothy stepped out of the pilothouse and motioned to Ida and Beth. They both got up from their spots out on the bow and came in. Dorothy pointed to the map. "Just as we turn, you'll be able to see Sansum Narrows. The current will pick up a little, but it's quite safe."

Everyone was quiet as they passed through the narrows. Dorothy pointed to the right. "That's Salt Springs Island over there, and opposite is Maple Bay on the mainland. See up ahead? That's Maple Bay."

Beth smiled at Ida as Dorothy continued as travel guide, even though she had never been to any of the places she pointed out. She read along in the guidebook, looked at the map, raised her head and looked around, and then announced the landmarks. "You'll be able to see Crofton soon because of the smokestacks—they have a paper mill there—and when we get Chemainus, we'll be about halfway." She put her hand on the wine bottle in the cabinet as Paul reached for it. Glaring at him, she shook her head. "You girls are welcome to ride up here in the pilothouse." She patted the foam-covered bench behind her and arranged some pillows. The miles passed quietly to the steady hum of the diesel engine and the blue luster of the quiet, sun-drenched water. Dorothy brought sandwiches and tea for lunch, and a box of chocolate cookies an hour later. Hypnotized by the sound and the glare, Ida and Beth dozed with their eyes half open, the sun flashing in and out from behind billowy white clouds. The breeze picked up a little, and *Destiny* slapped one-to-two foot waves as they approached Chemainus. Dorothy pointed. "There's Chemainus on the left and that's Thetis Island on the right. We're going to go through here. That's Ladysmith up ahead on the left, and you can see Yellow Point straight ahead. That's where we're going." Dorothy saw Paul's head slump and then snap up. "Ida, Beth, would you girls like to drive for a while? I think Paul needs a little nap."

Ida shrugged. "Sure. So we just head to that point of land way up there?"

"That's it. Keep the compass at about three hundred fifty degrees or just watch that point. We'll go by there."

Paul got off the seat. "It's all yours. Wake me up when you get close to Yellow Point. Dorothy, you'll be watching, right?"

"I'll be right here with them."

Paul clumped down the stairs, and Dorothy turned to Beth, taking her arm. "He's been drinking all day. I don't know how he can see anything."

"Drinkers adapt," Beth said. "I might be out of line, but in my work we would call him a high-functioning alcoholic."

Dorothy nodded. "Well, he functions." She wiped her eyes with a tissue. "I thought retirement and this new boat would make a difference." She looked out at the passing clouds. "Now I'm frightened something is going to happen. This boat is a mistake."

Ida turned. "He seems happy enough. Maybe you can get him to taper off when he's driving or just travel in the mornings."

"What am I going to do? We can't go around this island without some help." She put her hand on a large map. "That's the Pacific Ocean out there. Paul doesn't have any experience."

Beth nodded. "Maybe you could get him to stay on the inside, you know, get to know the Gulf Islands, stay at marinas."

"Oh, I don't know. He's dead set on going to the west side."

They rode along in silence, Ida and Beth handing the binoculars back and forth, searching for eagles along the coastline.

"Stay about five kilometers out from Yellow Point. See over there? According to the map, that's really two islands, Ruxton and De Courcy. Ruxton Passage goes between them. Way in the distance is Gabriola Island, this long one. It's almost fourteen kilometers—nine miles long. See, if you take these dividers and put them on the scale, it's about ten kilometers to here, and then about four more to the end."

"Maybe you should be the captain," Ida said.

"Don't tell Paul, but secretly I am. I've been doing some defensive reading." Dorothy smiled. "I'm going to wake him up. He'll want to drive through Ruxton Passage. He wants to see Pirate's Cove."

Paul left the Stuart Channel and steered dead center through Ruxton Passage into Pylades Channel. He followed along the shoreline of De Courcy Island to a place about one kilometer off of the entrance to Pirates Cove, idled down the engine and shifted to neutral. *Destiny* rocked gently in the one-foot waves. "There it is. Pirate's Cove."

"It's a marine park," Dorothy said. She opened a guidebook. "It says here Brother XII came here in the nineteen twenties with his religious cohorts and may have buried gold bars on the island or down in the water. He had a woman named Madame Z who ran the settlement with an iron fist and a bullwhip. She didn't let other women near him. People brought him their life savings. Brother XII said he was the reincarnation of the Egyptian god Osiris—wow, what a swindler. They tried to get him in court in Nanaimo, but he and Madame Z escaped."

"Are we going into the cove? It looks really narrow."

"No, it's too shallow for me to drive in there. See how the sandbar comes out? That marker is on top of rocks. Let's just sit here for a while. It's a pretty place."

"You girls want a cold drink? A soda or something?"

"I'd like a cola," Ida said. "I know where they are—in the cooler on the swim platform, right? Besides, I need to use the head."

Ida came out of the head and walked out the back door to the deck. She put on her life jacket because that was Dorothy's rule—if you're outside, you have to wear your life jacket. She opened the three-foot high transom door and stepped onto the swim platform, holding onto a chrome safety rail. As she opened the strapped-down cooler, she heard the motor rev up as Paul backed up, water coming up over the swim platform. "Hey, I'm out here by the cooler," she shouted, grabbing the rail with both hands. "Hey, can anyone hear me?"

Beth stuck her head out the door of the pilothouse and saw Ida waving her hand. The motor drowned out her shouts. Beth stepped down three steps and then ran back up, waving at Paul and Dorothy. Paul looked at Beth and cringed as Dorothy shouted. He shifted to forward, making *Destiny* lurch, banging Ida's head on the flagpole and tossing her off the swim platform and into *Destiny*'s churning wash from the prop and the waves. Paul shifted back into neutral, but *Destiny* was already ten meters ahead of Ida.

The 52-degree water drew a gasping breath from Ida as her life jacket inflated, popping her head up out of the water. She inhaled foamy salt water and air, coughing and spitting. The cold wrapped around her as though she had broken through the ice on a frozen pond. In the haze, she imagined a fevered little baby being lowered into an ice water bath in the ICU. She could barely catch her breath, and she was dizzy from the bump on the back of her head. The cold burrowed through the back of her neck, fomenting memories and making her head shake, like that time years ago at the lake when she was 12.

Mom had persuaded her to go on an overnight camping trip to El Vado Lake with the youth group at church. A week before, Mom had taken her to the women's department at Sears to get her first bra. She remembered feeling mousy and embarrassed as the saleswoman commented about her early, robust development and said it was high time she had a proper bra. Mom and the saleswoman fussed over her with different sizes, and then Mom took her into a dressing room and tried a couple of them over her T-shirt. She picked one, had Ida take off her shirt, and fit her carefully, showing her how to adjust the straps. She wore the bra on the camping trip, along with prominent braces on her teeth and bumpy acne on her face. She covered her forehead with a swoop of blond hair, kept her lips puffed over her braces, and wore a jacket over a loose camping shirt she borrowed from Pop. It was April, and all twelve kids bundled up and took a ride on a pontoon boat. They were almost halfway across the lake when the boat began leaning to one side, its pontoon filling with water. It sunk down to where the deck was flooded, and the outboard motor sputtered and died. The wind was brisk, and rain clouds hovered on the horizon. All of a sudden, a 25 mph gust of wind hit them, and kids began slipping and sliding, some, including Ida, slipping into the icy water.

From the shore, people saw what was happening, and three small aluminum fishing boats motored through the waves and began picking up the kids. They were cold, wet, and frightened. Ida remembered shivering, her teeth chattering, all the way back to the shore. As the kids got out of the boats, the youth sponsors helped them take off life jackets, sweaters, and jackets, wrapping them in blankets and sleeping bags. A young man with blond hair and a blue cap helped Ida with her life jacket and camping jacket. The next moment arose in her mind like a glaring light in the night. He stopped helping. He stared at the wet, light beige camping shirt plastered against her drooping bra and her puffed-out cleavage. His jaw dropped. "Wow, Ida. I didn't realize how fast you're growing up." Ida's eyes opened wide and she turned bright pink. Several boys looked at her, nudging one another, giggling, and then one of the wide-eyed fathers stared at her with something strange in his eyes. A surge of warmth she did not understand drove her shivering away, pressed into the small of her back, straightened her shoulders, and made her stand tall, her pink face and green eyes meeting the man's lusty stare—a stare she would come to know later as a source of strength. A woman stepped up and quickly covered Ida with a brown wool Army surplus blanket. She glanced at the man with a frown, and then frowned at all the young boys. Until now, Ida had never been immersed in water so cold, and yet on that day, her young skin tingled with fresh heat from a man's desire.

A yellow inflated ring hit Ida in the face. "Grab onto that," Beth said. "Put your head and arms through it. I'll pull you in." Ida moved slowly, numb from the cold. She pulled the ring over her head and stuck one arm through. The other arm was too heavy to lift. She began shivering violently. "Hold on," Beth said. She slowly dragged Ida through the small, choppy waves. Dorothy coiled the line as Beth pulled Ida up to the starboard side of the swim platform. She and Dorothy slid her up on the platform and then dragged her through the transom door and onto the deck. Beth peeled off her life jacket and her jersey vest. Then she pulled off Ida's gray hoodie sweatshirt. Ida moved one arm, pointing toward Paul. "I don't have a bra." Dorothy wrapped two blankets around her, leaning Ida against the back wall. "I'll get some hot tea," Dorothy said.

Paul clumped down the steps. "Everyone okay?"

Ida whispered into Beth's ear. "Ida wants to know why the hell you backed up. She was on the swim platform."

"We were drifting too close to shore. I was just backing up a little. Sorry."

Ida stood up, and Beth helped her inside and then on to the couch. "Just rest. Take some deep breaths." Dorothy brought a cup of tea with a little brandy in it. "Drink this. It'll warm you up."

Beth helped Ida into a warm shower and dry clothes. "I'm doing much better." She nibbled at some cheddar cheese and crackers. "Thanks for your help. I was frightened."

Dorothy went up to the pilothouse. Paul slipped *Destiny* into gear; they headed slowly toward Gabriola Pass, sometimes a treacherous place, and they were approaching on the flood tide, not a good idea if the current was running fast. Paul didn't check tides or currents. Dorothy put her hand on his. "Maybe we should wait for a while. It's the flood tide, and the water is speeding up."

"It'll be okay. I'll aim for the center."

"We should just drift out here for a while. The guidebook advises boats to wait for slack or the ebb. I'll make some soup. Wouldn't you like some chicken soup?"

"Relax. *Destiny* has three hundred seventy horsepower." Paul hunched up in his captain's chair and steered a course to the center of the pass. As he approached, the flood current started pushing *Destiny*, and the closer he got, the faster the current pushed. He backed off the throttle, but his speed over ground was still nine knots, and he had very little steering control. He turned the wheel and applied power, and *Destiny* started turning broadside to the pass. He spun the wheel the other way and corrected, but *Destiny* gained speed, and his face turned white as he wiped his forehead with a towel. He could see submerged rocks on his port side, and he scrunched his shoulders and buttocks. Within seconds, the surging, frothy water slammed *Destiny* through the pass and out the other side. Paul applied power and turned to his port, aiming at the channel behind the Breakwater Island, the rocky island that separated the pass from the Georgia Strait. He took a breath and glanced at Dorothy. "Piece of cake. *Destiny* is a great boat."

Within a half hour, Paul pulled into Silva Bay. On the radio, the harbormaster directed him to slip B19, a portside tie. There was no other boat in B20, so Paul turned in the spot. He came in too fast, and *Destiny*'s bow smacked the dock. He backed up, came forward again, and let *Destiny*'s fenders bump the dock, making an eerie creaking sound. People sitting outside at the pub stood up to watch. Beth jumped out and secured the bow to a cleat. Paul pulled the stern in with the thruster, and Ida jumped out and tied the stern cleat. Dorothy unrolled the yellow electrical cable and plugged it in. "I've got power," Paul said. He shut down the engine and poured himself a coffee cup full of wine. Dorothy waved at him. "Let's go eat. The guidebook says the Silva Bay Pub and Restaurant has great food." People smiled as Beth and Ida walked by. Ida smiled back and shrugged her shoulders.

After cheeseburgers and home fries at the restaurant, Ida and Beth left Dorothy and Paul at the table and walked up and down the dock checking out the boats and watching the night gather on the water and the rocky shore. A Border Patrol boat was tied up at the end, and sailboats were packed in the slips like sardines. There were several high-priced tugboats and two yachts side by side with a group of people playing cards and laughing—probably traveling together. The tide was ebbing and slowing down as darkness covered the bay. The dock lights came on as Ida turned to Beth. "I think this is a mistake. I didn't feel safe with Paul drinking all day. He's a mess. I could've drowned." Beth shook her head. "I was scared back there at the pass. The docking part is embarrassing. I'm getting tired of him yelling at us."

"I looked at the maps. We could ask them to let us off at Nanaimo and rent a car."

"I was thinking about that too. I'd feel guilty leaving Dorothy with Paul still in that boot and on his crutch."

"Guilty or not, can we handle another three days?"

"There's a lot of open water tomorrow. Maybe we can talk Paul into letting us drive."

Beth ran her fingers through her hair. "I'm going to get my shampoo and go up for a shower. They have washers and dryers if you want to do some laundry later. There's recycle bins out in back."

"You've been here before?"

"I've been almost everywhere in the Gulf Islands and on Vancouver

Island. I have a lot of years here." Beth smiled. "See you in a while. Meet you back at *Destiny*."

Ida walked the docks for a while, and then stepped aboard *Destiny* and gathered up enough clothes and towels for a load of laundry. She took a handful of change out of a cup in the silverware drawer. Paul had drifted off to sleep on the sofa, and Dorothy was up on the flybridge smoking. Ida stepped back on the dock, walked up behind the restaurant to the laundry room, and started a washer load. She heard the shower running in the next room and a man and a woman giggling. The dryers, chairs, and magazines were adjacent to the showers, so Ida took a seat and paged through a recent *Vancouver Sun*, intrigued by the gentle laughter and then the watery gasps of passion.

Ida turned her head away, but then snapped back as Beth and Greg stepped out of the shower, throwing open the curtain to the dressing area. Greg grabbed a towel. "Oops, didn't realize anyone else was here."

She stood dripping wet, hands on her hips, giggling, jiggling. "Now here's a coincidence, eh? Could you please toss me one of those towels?"

Ida stood up and handed Beth a towel, staring at her beautiful, proportioned body. The buzzing florescent light made her wet skin gleam with youth. Her breasts were firmer than her age, and lean muscles stood out on her arms and shoulders. Her shapely thighs and calves made her look 15 years younger. Ida was stunned by how comfortable Beth appeared, naked and beautiful, dripping wet and relaxed. Her stance was not sexy, but statuesque—a classic expression of the female form. Ida handed her a light blue towel. "Yes, I'd say it's a coincidence. How are you, Greg?"

He faced Ida with his hands on his hips, his body beaded with water. "Doing fine. Heard you might be staying at Silva Bay, so I came to visit. Had to check out some tourists anyway." He turned his back and pulled on some white boxer shorts.

10

*P*aul drove *Destiny* out of Silva Bay, passed Entrance Island on the inside, and set a line-of-sight course to the southern tip of Lasqueti Island, keeping well outside the Winchelsea Island group. Paul forgot to turn on his radio. It was a cool, partly cloudy day, and the sun peeked through the clouds sparkling in the occasional whitecaps on the two-foot waves. Ida sat in a deck chair on the bow in her green sweats and yellow rain jacket with binoculars and a mug of coffee. The rhythm of the bow breaking the waves lulled her into a somnolent state, halfway between awake and asleep, a reverie. She watched the clouds form shapes and move northerly in the breeze of the upper air. One puffy gray cloud took on the shape of her mother, a soft, wispy hand taking her arm, pulling her across the parking lot, and pushing her into the church for youth group.

Ida remembered Mom taking her into the women's bathroom, arranging her clothes, buttoning her blouse, smoothing her bra straps, and straightening her loose denim jeans. "There, now, that's the proper way to dress for church activities. You're growing up too soon, Ida, and for some reason God has given you this body. You must learn to be modest."

"Mom, why do you worry? I know how to take care of myself."

They went into the hallway, and Mom turned to leave. "I'll be back at nine thirty. Have you got your Bible?"

"Yes, in my bag, and I've got a hymnal and my sweater."

"Okay then, have a good time."

Ida went back into the women's room and locked herself in a stall. She changed clothes into a pink push-up bra and a fitted white sweater with a green scarf draped around her neck. That was her drill, changing clothes every time. She would change back at 9:15 pm and meet Mom at the outside door. Kevin, the youth director, grinned broadly as she walked into the youth room. She moved toward him with a little sway, meeting his eyes, but appearing blank and unaware of her impact, leaving him guessing what was behind her clear green eyes and her push-up bra, the pink color clearly visible. Ida had developed the fine art of exposing herself a little more than expected, but never arising to what Mom called flaunting. She could tell she was riding on the edge by watching the turned heads and extended glances of the men as she walked by. At age 13, her green innocent eyes and her nubile curves had created an aura of magnetism, a smoky haze that surrounded her. Along with her smell of jasmine and spicy amber, this was the persona she inhabited, the persona that bolstered her self-confidence, the persona that directed her through her teen years, generated her power, warmed her insecure soul, attracted older boys, and got her kicked out of the youth group. The other mothers conspired to have Ida move out of youth activities before she was 14, but they never talked about it. Ida's provocative lure, unspoken and mysterious, ran just under the surface of any discussion, deep enough where no one could point it out and risk offending Mom—the Hospitality Chairwoman for the church. Mom didn't object when Ida joined the cheerleading team at school, even though she wore short skirts, probably because there were fewer boys, and she was involved in sports, an acceptable activity in the Corley household.

She chose Kevin at a weekend retreat for her first sexual encounter. It happened in a tent in the middle of the night on a red air mattress that smelled like new plastic. Kevin was awkward the way he poked around, probably because he felt guilty about his 19 years pushing into her 13 years, but Ida spread her legs farther than he imagined she could; she welcomed him with little murmurs and cries, and then pulled him out and rubbed on him until he sighed and dripped all over his sleeping bag. Ida stood up naked while Kevin watched her dress. She slipped on her white T-shirt, pink bikini panties, white shorts, and crawled out of the tent. She remembered Kevin that way, and the way he was when they met two other times in the back of his '78 Dodge Charger. They had to climb over the seats to get in back, and she left him both times on his back, dripping. Even at 13, she knew enough to keep those little sperm out of there. She remembered a little sadness when Kevin moved away that summer. He was a nice boy, the beginning of her secret life, far from the suspicions of her mother, a gateway to the desires of men that filled an empty place and, like a drug, eased her troubled soul.

Ida's sleepy reverie stopped abruptly as the huge profile of a Navy battleship appeared. A red Coast Guard Zodiac with four men aboard slapped through the waves toward *Destiny*. Ida looked up to the pilothouse where Paul seemed to be dozing. Dorothy shook his shoulder and pointed at the arriving boat. Paul throttled down and slipped *Destiny* into neutral. The Zodiac powered down and bumped the side of *Destiny*. One man held a megaphone to his mouth. "Turn on your radio, your radio." Another man tied a line to one of *Destiny*'s cleats, and three armed men came aboard, one stepping toward Ida. "Where's your captain?"

Ida pointed at the windshield as Paul and Dorothy stepped out the side door. Paul leaned on the rail. "What the hell's the matter, mate?"

"We've been hailing your for twenty minutes. Is your radio off?"

Paul looked back inside, then reached in and snapped the radio on. "It's on now. What did we do?"

"You're in Whisky Gulf, a restricted military area. Don't you have charts?"

"I've got a map. We're headed straight up there toward Lasqueti Island."

"Not any more." One man climbed up the stairs, and the other two began searching *Destiny*. Beth smiled at the two other patrol officers as they pawed through drawers and cabinets, searching through the galley, the head, and the bedrooms. They even dug around in the dirty laundry before they went back out on the bow deck. Both men looked at Ida. "Are you Canadian?"

"No, I'm from the US, Albuquerque, New Mexico. I'm here as a tourist."

"Do you have your passport?"

"Just a moment." Ida went into the cabin, opened her roller bag, and came back with her papers. "Here's my passport and my driver's license."

The patrol officer looked them over, held Ida's passport photo up to her face, and then handed them back to her. "Are you related to these folks?"

"No, my friend and I are riding with them up to Alert Bay. I'm looking for someone who's up there doing research on killer whales. He teaches at UBC."

"That's where the whales are—good luck. Hey, this captain needs some education."

The patrol officer walked up on the flybridge, and then stepped down, moving into the pilothouse. "Do you have a guidebook?"

Dorothy produced the Gulf Island guidebook, and the officer opened it to the inside of the front cover. "See here? You're in the gray zone, Whisky Gulf, and today it's active. You need to move east, over here by the Winchelseas and follow this line up the Ballenas channel past Ballenas Island. Then you can turn toward Lasqueti. My God, Captain, we could impound your boat for this. Are you a new captain?"

"Just got the boat two months ago. This is our first trip out of Sidney."

"I smell alcohol. Have you been drinking?"

"Had a little nip in my coffee. That's probably what you smell."

The officer shook his head. "Get yourself some better charts. There are many hazards in the Gulf Islands. Tell you what. We'll give you one chance to get out of this area and stay out. Keep your radio on. I'm going to hail you in an hour or so." He looked at the two other patrol officers. They motioned toward the Zodiac, and they all three boarded and cast the line loose.

The man held up his megaphone. "Get on with it. Get going."

Paul scrambled into the pilothouse, shifted into gear, turned sharp to port, and headed in a straight line to a group of islands in the distance.

Dorothy stood next to Paul. "You need to pay better attention. Look, here's a sketch of where we are going. You need to go around here to get into the channel." Dorothy used a yellow marker to highlight the route. Paul narrowed his eyes, speeded up to 10 knots, and gritted his teeth. "Who the hell do they think they are anyway?"

"The Coast Guard—and they don't mess around. We're lucky they let us go."

Beth and Ida came up the stairs to the pilothouse with fresh coffee for everyone. Ida handed Paul a mug, and then looked at the guidebook. "Where are we now?"

Dorothy used a set of dividers and pointed. "We're right about here, and we can look straight out there and see Winchelsea Island. We're going to the south of the island." She traced the route on the guidebook map. "Then we go by Ada Island, turn right, and head north until we're past Whisky Gulf. See, it's crosshatched. Look out there. You can see Nanoose Bay in the distance."

Ida scanned the horizon through her binoculars. This whole fiasco had set them back a couple of hours. That Coast Guard guy was well built, but he seemed a little too tough. She barely caught a glimmer of his interest as he held her passport up to her face. Maybe he was gay.

Paul followed the path Dorothy drew, passed Winchelsea Island, and approached Ada Channel. It was about two pm, and the flood tide had started to come in, just covering the rocks near Ada, rocks that were exposed at slack tide. Paul stayed 50 meters south of Ada, slowed to about five knots, and got ready to make his turn. That's when it happened. *Destiny*'s keel whacked a submerged rock, making a grinding sound, and the boat started to vibrate. Paul cut the power and slipped it into neutral. Dorothy slapped her forehead. "What in the world was that?"

"I don't know. Maybe we hit something."

"Oh, that's all we need," Ida said.

"I'm following Dorothy's line—I don't know what happened."

Paul put *Destiny* into gear and applied power. *Destiny* shook and vibrated. He backed off the power and put it back into neutral. He applied power. No vibration in neutral. He tried again, and *Destiny* shook. "It feels like the prop is bent. I think it's making the whole boat shake."

Ida crossed her arms, frowning. "Now what, Captain Paul?"

Paul grabbed the guidebook and looked in the index. He took his cell phone out of his pocket and dialed. "Hello, is this Vessel Assist? I'm Paul McHugh and my membership number is B-twenty thirty-seven. I'm the captain of the motor vessel *Destiny*."

"How can I help you, Captain?"

"I think I hit a rock. When I power up, the boat shakes."

"I've got you here on the computer. You're a forty-two foot North Pacific, right?"

"Yes sir."

"Single engine diesel?"

"Yup, three hundred seventy horsepower."

"Drop the rpm down to an idle and slip it into gear."

"Okay. The vibration is really strong."

"You've got a bow thruster?"

"Yes, I've got bow thruster and a stern thruster."

"Okay, leave the engine running at idle. That'll keep the batteries charged. You can use your thrusters to keep your position. I'll send a boat out. We're going to have to tow you into Schooner Bay in Nanoose Bay or back to Nanaimo. My guess is Nanaimo will be the only place we can get parts and get you hauled out."

"How far is that?"

"Nanaimo is about twenty kilometers from Ada. We can have you there in three or four hours."

"How long do you think the repairs will take?"

"I'll call ahead to schedule the haul-out. They won't know until they check. If you need a new prop, they'll have to fly one in from Vancouver. I'd guess a day or two. There are some nice motels within walking distance. I'd say if you have to be stranded for a while, Nanaimo's as good a place as you'll find."

The Vessel Assist boat arrived in half an hour, hooked up a towline, and headed for Nanaimo. The trip took four hours, and they tied up at the boatyard. They packed a few clothes and toiletries in roller bags, went ashore, and arranged a ride with the Vessel Assist people to the Buccaneer Motel, a two-story clean white building on the east side of Stewart Avenue. As they turned onto Stewart from the boat yard, Beth motioned to her right. "There's Nauticals, one of the best restaurants in Nanaimo. We'll walk back here for dinner. The fish and chips are scrumptious."

"The guidebook says Nauticals has a four-star rating," Dorothy said.

They were dropped off at the check-in door, and Paul put his credit card down for two rooms on the ground floor. "Not sure how long we'll be here," he said. "Maybe only two nights."

Ida and Beth unpacked, used the bathroom, and opened a bottle of wine Beth brought from *Destiny*. "Let's relax a minute," Ida said. "I'm uneasy about this whole *Destiny* thing."

"Sure. It's just a ten-minute walk. We can be there before dark and get a table on the back deck." They sat at the table looking out the window at the ferry in the distance. Beth held up her plastic cup. "Cheers."

Ida touched her cup to Beth's, drained her cup, and stood up. She ran a brush through her hair and retied her ponytail. "Let's go. I'm hungry."

They crossed Stewart Avenue, turned right, and walked along the shore walkway. Beth pointed. "That's the ferry dock three blocks behind us, and that's Newcastle Island just across the water. It's a beautiful park."

They went into Nauticals. Paul was sitting at the bar, and Dorothy was sitting in the wait area by the door. "Oh, there you are. Paul and I came on ahead."

They asked for a table out on the back deck and ordered fish and chips and a pint. "Beer tastes good with the fish," Dorothy said.

Ida ate quietly for a few minutes, took a breath, and put her hand on Dorothy's arm. "This isn't at all what we expected. I'm thinking about renting a car in the morning. We can be in Alert Bay by tomorrow night."

"I guess I wouldn't blame you. We could stay here for a week or so until Paul is out of his boot." She put her head down and then looked at Beth. "I'm afraid, afraid something bad is going to happen—I have a sense of impending doom."

"I understand. Paul is unpredictable, but you're doing a good job filling in with the guidebook and everything. If he'll listen to you, I think you'll do okay."

"When things go bad, I've seen Paul just throw up his hands and get drunk, no matter what's going on around him. He's more fragile than you think."

On the way back to the Buccaneer, Ida stopped by a pay phone. "I'm going to call Danny. You guys go on ahead." She used a phone card.

"Ida, what a great surprise. Where are you?"

Ida told him the story about Whiskey Gulf, the Coast Guard, hitting the rocks by Ada Island, and the tow to Nanaimo. "The Buccaneer is a nice motel, right by the water. We're planning on renting a car tomorrow. This boat travel isn't working out."

"I miss you, Ida. I've got a few days off. I thought I might put Jedi and ER in the kennel and fly up there to be with you. I can get to Seattle tomorrow. They probably have a flight to Nanaimo. Shall I check?"

Ida rubbed the back of her neck. It would be nice to see him—she could get an extra room, he could drive with them, but then she'd have to explain who he was. Could be awkward. He'd want to take over, and that would piss her off. Two women alone would find out more, faster. Joel was going to be on edge, anyway. Adding another man...

"I think Beth and I ought to go by ourselves. I should be home in a week or so anyway."

"I'm crazy without you."

"And, you're crazy with me."

"Love you."

"Danny, I really need my space right now."

"Got it. Your space. No problem."

"Bye."

Ida paged through the phone book, called a car rental agency, and booked a 2004 Chevrolet for the trip to Cormorant Island. They would have to drive to Port McNeill to drop off the car and then take the ferry to Alert Bay. She walked back to the Buccaneer and told Beth.

Beth nodded her head. "I've been thinking, and I'm worried Dorothy is on the edge of a major depression. Maybe we could spend some time with her tomorrow, help her get ready for the rest of their trip—it would only delay us a day."

"They're both so impossible. It's all I can do."

"I know, but think about it. What if he was in the ICU at your hospital? You'd sit with her in the waiting room, right?"

"Oh, of course I would. But I'm on this mission—getting there, finding Joel. Maybe I'm not thinking straight."

"Over the years, I've normally been thrown together with people for a reason. Usually there's something I can do. We met each other randomly on a whale-watching boat, and here we are with Dorothy and Paul. Don't you think there might be a reason?"

Ida stood up and began to pace around the room. "What did you have in mind?"

"Paul will be occupied with the haul-out and the mechanics. We could take Dorothy somewhere for the day, you know, just be her friends."

"I guess one day wouldn't hurt."

Beth unfolded a map of Newcastle Island. "These hiking trails wander through the trees, and you can see the ocean. We can pick up a few things at the store. The little ferry runs all day, so we can be back by evening."

Ida crossed her arms, glanced beside her, and saw herself in the mirror. Her features seemed harsh. She was a nurse after all. She cared about people. Patients said she brought a healing presence—they could feel it when she was in their rooms. She took a breath. "You're right. I'll call the rental agency and put off the car for a day. Where's Dorothy now?"

"She's sitting outside by herself. I'll go tell her we've made plans."

In the morning they took the little ferry to Newcastle Island, sat by the beach for a while, ate peach yogurt with granola, stopped up at the bathroom, and then started off on the trail around the island, pausing at view points along the way. From the cliff, Ida shaded her eyes with her hand, looked out into the Strait, and then peered through her binoculars. "Hey, Beth, I can see whales. Come look." She handed the binoculars to Beth.

"There's three of them, coming this way. I think I see Mike." Ida took the binoculars.

"It is. It's Mike, Slick, and Alki. There's four or five behind them about three-hundred meters. Whoa, it looks like Mike is spyhopping. He's way out there."

Ida took a breath, handed the binoculars back to Beth, stretched out her arms, and flopped on her back. The pine needles made a soft, crisp-smelling bed, and she closed her eyes. The breeze stirred the strong scent of fir trees; the smells took her back to the pine-scented spray cleaner Mom used on the stainless steel countertops in the church kitchen. She remembered Mom baking pies for Junior and for church one weekend, whispering and crying with her friend about Junior's drinking. Junior was thirty and lived in a mobile home out behind the Corley's main house. Mom wiped her eyes, telling her friend that she felt helpless and couldn't do anything about Junior's drinking. He blamed her; she lived in fear he would hurt himself and, angry, wishing he would, but helped him every day with food and laundry. The rehab counselor had laughed about that later in the family meetings. The family later came to see alcoholism as a family disease, and Mom played her part enabling. Junior's recovery had been remarkable. He asked Mom to forgive him for all the grief he had caused her. Mom reacted with gentle compassion.

Ida smelled Beth's lavender perfume as she sat down beside her, handing her the binoculars. "Mike is still coming this way. He's only about one kilometer out. Slick and Alki are hanging back. Maybe he knows you're up here."

"Maybe. I'll try to send him a message." She closed her eyes. Her head swayed back and forth, and she smiled.

"What did you tell him?"

Ida laughed. "This is silly, but I said we'd probably be back in the water soon, heading north, just like he told us."

"So you're going to be okay with Paul and the boat?"

"Dorothy probably needs us. My brother was like Paul. Alcoholism is tough on everyone."

They caught up with Dorothy, walked awhile, and then stopped at a quiet place in the trees.

Beth sat beside Dorothy on a fallen fir tree log. "I remember you said you have two grown children, right?"

"Yes, Kevin and Lonnie. Kevin is forty-two—he's a nurse, like you, Ida, but he's at a drug and alcohol rehab center in Toronto. Lonnie is forty and an art teacher in Montreal."

"Do you have any grandchildren?"

"No, Kevin is still single, and Lonnie lives with her partner Veronica."

"You must be proud, a registered nurse and a teacher."

"We usually see them at Christmas. Kevin goes to Lonnie's place and Montreal, and we see them there. We missed this past Christmas, though. Paul was sick, and Kevin had to work, so it didn't work out."

"I've never had children. It must be nice."

"Sometimes. It can be sad. They left home when they went off to college, and they've been on their own since. Lonnie always sends birthday cards." Dorothy stood up and swung her daypack over her shoulder. "I guess we should keep on going, eh?"

Beth and Ida fell in behind Dorothy. She was trudging, a labored stride, as if she was pulling a long burden behind her, tipping her head forward as though someone had harnessed her shoulders to a horse-drawn plow. After another kilometer, she stopped and sat on another log. She glanced at Beth. "I don't know how much longer I can take it."

Her gray-blue eyes were dull. Beth surmised Dorothy's efforts in her marriage had drawn filmy shades over the blue in her eyes, leaving them mostly gray. "What can't you take?"

"All of it. Marriage, Paul, this boat, my children—they really have disappointed me. They just went away. Lonnie said she never wanted to see Vancouver again, and Kevin says he's the happiest when he's alone."

"Sound like you've been sad for some time. Have you talked with anyone about it?"

"What good would that do? I don't want to complain. I just want it to go away—everything is so dark. I don't enjoy anything any more."

"Do you have any hobbies?"

"I used to like my garden, but now we're on a boat. Paul wants to live aboard until October, way past the growing season. It's his drinking, you know. If I could only get him to stop."

"You don't have much control over that."

Dorothy wiped her eyes with her sleeve, stood up, and hurried down the trail.

Ida jogged, caught up to Dorothy, and walked beside her. "Do you have any friends or relatives on Vancouver Island?"

Dorothy slowed her pace. "I have an older sister in Port Hardy, way up north. Her husband's a fisherman. They have a little grocery store."

"Do you ever get to see her?"

"We used to write, but now we send emails. Not really much to say. She says I should lay down the law, tell Paul to quit or get out. Says I should have left him years ago."

"That's hard to do, especially when you love someone."

Dorothy nodded. "I keep hoping something will happen, but it keeps getting darker."

"Could you visit your sister for a while? Maybe Paul could go on a fishing trip and you could stay with her and get a break."

"Mary Lou wouldn't mind. She's always ready to take care of me, but I don't want anybody to take care of me. Everything's so confusing. I just want to be alone."

Dorothy picked up her pace. Ida and Beth followed about 20 meters behind for the next two kilometers. They stopped at a lookout, had some lunch, finished their walk around the island, hopped on the ferry, and then walked back to the Buccaneer. Dorothy opened her door quietly. "Paul's asleep. I'll read for a while. We can get some dinner about eight, okay?"

"Sure," Beth said.

"Wait a minute. Here's a note. Paul says the boat is ready and we can leave in the morning."

Beth nodded as Dorothy closed the door. She and Ida walked down Stewart, sat on a park bench by an array of crimson flowers, and watched the BC Ferry come in. "I don't have the heart to leave her alone with Paul on the boat, do you?"

Ida pursed her lips. "No, she needs us."

"Let's see if we can get her to check in with her sister."

"I'll call and cancel the car. I guess I can stand a couple more days."

As they walked back to the Buccaneer, Beth suddenly quickened her step and waved at a Border Patrol SUV. Greg Bartley was parked just off Stewart in the parking lot. "Look, Ida, it's Greg."

He was leaning against the driver's side door talking on a portable radio. As they approached, Greg grinned and clipped the radio onto his belt. "Hey, I got your call. I helped with the ferry check-in from Horseshoe Bay. The Coastal Renaissance ran an hour late."

"We've been down at the Departure Bay. I guess I didn't see your SUV," Beth said.

Ida crossed her arms. "Hello, Greg. You seem to show up everywhere."

"It's a small island, ma'am. Besides, I'm sort of watching out for you."

"You can call me Ida."

Greg tipped his hat. "Yes, ma'am."

Beth raised her eyebrows and smiled at Ida. "There's a bookstore nearby called the Good Old Book Exchange. You said earlier you are a collector, and they specialize in rare books."

"Which way do I go?"

Greg pointed. "Go south on Stewart to Hemlock, then east to Terminal Avenue. In a block or so you'll come to Estevan, and it's right there in that shopping center—right between Blockbuster Video and Canada Trust. It's about a twenty minute walk."

Ida turned and adjusted her backpack. "I'll see you in a couple of hours." After a few steps, Ida looked over her shoulder. Beth was already opening the door to their room.

The bookstore was fascinating and Ida lost track of time as she looked through the first editions. The old books smelled like musty paper and leather, and they gave off a sense of stability that soothed Ida's annoyance. What was this ma'am stuff? Hell, Beth was almost 20 years older than her, and she was Greg's age. She had lifted her eyes to him and he didn't seem to notice. A title jumped out at her from a glass case—Steinbeck's *The Pearl*. Ida motioned to a clerk, who unlocked the case. "This one is the nineteen forty-seven first edition, and the dust cover is torn at the bottom of the spine." He handed the book to Ida. She had been looking for *The Pearl* for years, but hadn't found one with a dust jacket. The Brodart plastic book jacket cover felt new and crisp.

She opened it carefully. "Any chance it's signed?"

"Sorry, afraid not."

"How much are you asking?"

"It's a tight copy, probably hasn't been read. The dust jacket is faded some, and there are some tears...say, three hundred dollars? That's a good price."

"Would you take two-fifty and ship it to my home in Albuquerque?"

"It would have to go FedEx. Let's say three hundred and we'll pay the shipping."

"Okay, sold. I'll come up to the counter in a little while."

Ida wandered the store, jubilant, as though her first edition *The Pearl* was a sign that her future had brightened. A surge of compassion for Dorothy led her to the contemporary fiction area, and she located a paperback copy of William Styron's *Darkness Visible*—the story of his journey through depression and the hope he found. Maybe Dorothy would find it helpful. As she wandered past the sex and self-help books, she spied a brightly colored paperback copy of *The Kama Sutra of Vatsyayana*. She smiled to herself as she thought about buying it for Beth—no, that would be too cheeky.

11

On the morning, *Destiny* and crew made headway north again, and stayed inside the Winchelseas and the Ballenas islands. Their route took them between Denman and Hornby islands, and as they got past Cape Lazo, Dorothy told Paul to cross Georgia Strait so they could visit the village of Lund, the last stop at the end of the road on the mainland. She wanted to tour the Lund Hotel and Nancy's Bakery, which, according to the guidebook, featured five-star bakery goods and an early morning cinnamon roll to die for ("You can't go wrong with anything at Nancy's"). They would stay overnight at the Lund Marina, then take off early in the morning. It was rare for Dorothy to assert herself, so Paul smiled and nodded. "Sounds like a good idea. Weather is nice enough." He turned *Destiny* slowly to starboard and headed to Savary Island, far in the distance, a crescent-shaped island with arbutus and Garry oak trees, and white sandy beaches. "We'll take it easy and stay at seven knots or so."

It was windy and sunny. There were a few whitecaps, but *Destiny* handled the waves easily. The girls went down to the galley. Paul set the autopilot and sipped coffee laced with brandy. It was nice to be alone, bouncing gently with the rhythm of the waves. He wondered how Kevin and Lonnie were doing. It was too bad they didn't care to visit any more, but they were too busy with their own lives. Sometimes he wished he could relive their early lives. He worked too much, and Dorothy said he drank too much. You're going to miss their growing up. First thing you know they'll be out of school and you will have missed it all. Maybe so, maybe he had missed a lot. All he knew to do was to work, to support his family, be available some on the weekends. He wasn't sure what it all meant. Forty years at the same company. He was a good engineer, and people all over British Columbia used the pumps and hydraulic valves he had designed. He had contributed financially and protected them from harm, but he was easily confused as a father. He was a man with all thumbs and a mind full of ideas he couldn't express to his son or his daughter. She said he was big-hearted and clueless; Lonnie said he was hapless. He tried for a while when they were younger, but they were both smart, and as soon as they entered school, they looked at him as though he was odd, perhaps even a stranger. He hated that look—a stranger to his own children—but he couldn't do anything about it. Would he do anything differently? Perhaps, but for the life of him, he couldn't imagine what it would be. While they were growing up, he sometimes asked Dorothy what to do. She said he should just talk with them. Tell them about his work or take them fishing. He remembered having fun at Stanley Park—the zoo and the aquarium. They both seemed to like Stanley Park. That was his last memory of having fun with them, and now, an unnamed regret had become his companion in retirement.

As Savary Island came into view, Paul carefully steered 500 meters to the south. He would pass by Savary, turn left, and have a straight shot to the Lund Marina. The wind picked up a little, so, fortunately, he slowed to about five knots so the boat could take the waves easier.

Did they leave after high school because of him? Dorothy got used to them being gone, but she was never the same. She used to hug him when the kids lived at home. He tried things like bringing home flowers and taking her to restaurants, but after a couple of months of things like that, he gave up. He cared about Dorothy, but sometimes she got on his nerves. Getting the boat was a great idea. It was something to do. He never meant any harm to his children. They had what they needed. He never uttered a harsh world to them. Better he should go somewhere by himself and have a pint. No sense making a scene.

Paul looked out the windshield with heavy-lidded eyes, and slowed down a little more. The water changed color to a light green. He saw some seaweed. Suddenly he hit bottom with a crunch and then felt a scraping slide as though he was on wet sand; then, abruptly, *Destiny* stopped dead in the water. His chest rammed the steering wheel as he fell forward. He shifted into neutral, killed the engine, took a couple of breaths, and then leaped down the stairs on his good leg. Dorothy had been slammed against the sink. Dishes, pans, cups, sandwiches, and chips had flown all over the floor. Ida was sprawled on the floor, thrown out of the easy chair; Beth cursed behind the door of the head. She had tumbled off the toilet. Dorothy glared at him. "What the hell happened?"

"I think we ran aground."

The tide was low, and Paul had run aground on sand, gravel, and seaweed on the bar between Savary and Mystery Reef, a notoriously dangerous place noted in all the guidebooks.

"You should've been up there with me reading the book and watching the map. I can't keep track of everything."

"So now it's my fault? I hate this boat."

Paul opened the floor hatch to the engine compartment. He shined a flashlight around. There was no water. He looked forward under the floor. No water. Seemed like the hull was in one piece. *Destiny* rocked side to side in the wind and waves, her keel firmly planted in the sand and gravel. He was lucky he missed any rocks. Everyone gathered themselves up and began picking up the litter. Beth changed her clothes.

Paul returned to the bridge. Red-faced and shaking, he called Vessel Assist again.

"Hello, *Destiny*. What is your location?"

"I'm about five hundred meters south of Savary Island, headed toward Lund."

"I see. Captain, look out to the south, on your starboard. Do you see a green can out there?"

"Yes, in the distance."

"That's Mystery Reef. Pretty sure you've run aground. Any water in your bilge?"

"No, I checked the engine compartment. The power is on to the bilge pumps, but they're not running."

"That's good. What was your speed when you went aground?"

"About three or four knots."

"I'm going to save you some money, Captain. It's just past slack tide at your location, and it is starting to flood, more than twelve feet by seven o'clock. Just sit tight. The tide should lift you off the gravel in a couple of hours. What is your destination for tonight?"

"The Lund Marina."

"You'll be fine. If the bilge pumps come on, Lund Marina has a diver that can look at your hull. Keep an eye on the engine compartment. Stay at one to two knots until you pass the edge of Savary on the east."

"Thanks. This was stupid of me."

"Lots of new boaters to the area take the shortcut. Sometimes they get through fine. It's a good idea to stay south of the green marker on Mystery Reef."

"Thanks, I'll make a note of it."

Within two hours, the tide had lifted *Destiny* off the gravel. Paul took it easy and pulled into the Lund Marina while it was still light. He hailed the harbormaster and asked for a slip.

"Sorry, *Destiny*, I don't have a single slip left inside the marina."

"Nothing at all?"

"Nope, I'm full up, but you're welcome to tie up on the outside, on the long dock. There's no power or water, and the waves can get rough."

Paul turned to Dorothy. "We can tie up there for the night. You can walk through the Lund Hotel, we can eat in the hotel restaurant, and we can go up to Nancy's Bakery in the morning."

"We don't have much choice, do we?"

"Guess not, unless we keep going. The guidebook shows anchorages in the Copeland Islands Marine Park—about five kilometers north."

Beth touched Dorothy's arm. "We'd better take what we can get, don't you think? We all need to stretch our legs. Let's have dinner at the hotel."

"Good idea," said Ida.

Ida and Beth dropped the fenders, Paul pulled up to the dock on the starboard side, and they secured a bow line, a stern line, and a breast line. Waves splashed against *Destiny*'s port side, making *Destiny* rock and the fenders squeak against the bleached gray wooden dock.

They ate juicy cheeseburgers, home fries and blueberry pie. Paul had several pints and stumbled back to the boat alone. The girls wandered around the area until the marina lights came on, and then ambled slowly to the boat.

"We have to remember Paul is sick," Beth said. "Alcoholism is a disease, and unfortunately these gaps in attention are symptoms. We can be angry if we want, but it's like being angry at someone who has allergies and sneezes all the time."

Dorothy stopped, shaking her head. "The other symptom is that Paul is an asshole—he treats me like dirt."

Ida laughed. "Well, there's that. We need a plan, don't you think? We need to gather forces."

Beth turned to Dorothy. "How about this—one of us will always be with him on the bridge, and we'll find reasons to stop soon after lunch. If we get up at daylight, we can travel for five or six hours. He seems to do best in the morning."

"Okay, I'll mark the route, and we'll make him follow it. I'll keep an eye on his drinking, like I always do. For all I care, he can get dead drunk after lunch. We'll be tied up in a marina or in an anchorage."

Destiny rolled and screeched against the dock all night long. No one slept except Paul, who was passed out, and in the gray daylight, three frowning, sleepy-eyed women made coffee, left it in the galley, jumped off the boat, and marched up to Nancy's Bakery. Dorothy brought back a cinnamon roll for Paul and tossed the white paper bag on his bed. "Wake up—it's time to get going."

12

*T*ired and irritable, Dorothy followed Paul to the pilothouse. Ida and Beth made ready to cast off from the Lund Marina outside dock. They were underway at 6:30 am, and Dorothy had already marked their route. Ida and Beth settled in next to Dorothy. It was rainy, gray, and chilly. A light wind blew from the southeast. Their travel day would take them to Quadra Island and then through Surge Narrows on the east side, a dangerous passage for *Destiny* if the current was running. Dorothy had studied the tide tables and the guidebook and, in order to be at Surge Narrows at slack tide, they needed to arrive at one pm, give or take a half hour. It was about 38 nautical miles, so Dorothy planned to average six-to-seven knots, an easy pace for *Destiny*. From there, they would travel another 18 miles through the Okisollo Channel and into Johnstone Strait as far as Chatham Point, where they would anchor for the night. If they went through the narrows at one pm, they should be at their anchorage by four. She sipped her coffee and turned to Paul.

"We have a plan."

"You do?"

"I've been studying the guidebook, Captain. Ida, Beth, and I are going to be your navigators, and I'm your first mate. Any problem with that?" Dorothy smiled at him.

Paul tipped his head, glancing at each of them. "No problem. It will make things easier if I don't have to worry about everything."

Dorothy opened the guidebook. "You'll be heading northwest to this location between Quadra and Read Island. Surge Narrows is right here. We need to average about six to seven knots, so hold her steady at seven knots." Dorothy turned the windshield wipers on.

Paul grinned. "Thanks, mate. I'll follow your marked route. How far is it?"

"About thirty-eight nautical miles," Beth said.

Ida leaned toward him. "We should be there about one."

Beth shuffled through a stack of CDs. "If it's okay with you, Captain, I'll put on some music—I like this *Alan Jackson Greatest Hits*." Paul nodded.

They supplied Paul with fresh coffee, drove while he took breaks for the head, and kept up an unceasing conversation in the pilothouse. Paul sipped a little brandy and ate the sandwiches and chips Dorothy provided.

About five miles out from Cortez Island, a fishing boat was on a course to cross their path. Paul pointed. "Check it out. Is that a fishing boat?"

Dorothy sorted through some other books, found another guide-book, and then thumbed through the pages identifying different types of boats. "That's an old troller. See those arms out to the sides? They're probably dragging ten lines and fishing for salmon."

"They're on a collision course with us. I'm going to slow down. I think the fishing boat has the right-of-way."

"Sure is an old rusty boat," Ida said. "Look, way behind—Orcas, four of them. Hey, there's a guy with a rifle."

Beth stood up, looking through the binoculars. "The fishermen think those Orcas are going to get their salmon. Probably trying to scare them off."

They could hear the sharp report of the rifle and then an echo. Ida watched the Orcas dive. "He's shooting at them. He's trying to kill them."

Paul stood up behind the wheel and peered through his binoculars. "You're right. That's a high-powered rifle, and they're only one hundred meters out." Paul turned the wheel, increased power, and aimed *Destiny* straight for the fishing boat, knowing he'd cross paths behind them over the trolling lines that were out. Two men waved their arms over their heads. Paul didn't slow down. "Those Orcas are innocent—they're just trying to eat. Those bastards don't have a right to kill them."

Ida's eyes opened wide. "What are you doing? We're going to crash."

"I'll make sure we pass behind them, out past where the lines go in the water. I want to get between that guy with the rifle and the Orcas. He won't shoot us."

Destiny's Caterpillar diesel whined, the fishing boat belched black diesel smoke out the stack, and *Destiny* slapped the waves, making 10 knots, bearing down on the other boat. Beth held on to her seat, and Ida grabbed a handhold overhead. Dorothy put one hand on the wheel and held onto Paul's belt with the other. They were 100 meters away and closing. Paul leaned on the horn, making one long blast and then pounded out a continuous staccato honk, honk, honk as he got closer. Dorothy turned white. "You're going to hit them. Are you crazy?"

"I can't let them shoot those killer whales." He closed in at 75 meters, 50 meters, and then at 25 meters Paul turned *Destiny* sharply to the starboard, making an arc of 180 degrees. *Destiny*'s wash rocked the fishing boat, the men shaking their fists and holding on to the rail. The rifle slid across the deck and lodged under a tangle of dock line. When he was 75 meters away, Paul slowed *Destiny* to four knots, slumped back into the captain's chair, and took some deep breaths. "I need a drink."

"I'll go get your brandy," Ida said.

Paul smiled, his hand on the red horn button. "I'm glad I bought the double air horn. Loud, eh? I thought it might come in handy." He turned to Dorothy. "Here, mate, take the wheel for a while and get us back on course. I'm going to hit the head."

Ida handed Paul his pint of brandy. After he trundled down the stairs, she put her hand on Dorothy's arm. "What was that all about?"

"I don't know. That was intense. I've never seen Paul arise to the defense of anyone but our children. He actually cared about those Orcas."

"He likely saved a life or two," Beth said. "That took courage."

They arrived at Surge Narrows a little before one pm. The tide was nearly slack, and a half-dozen boats lined up to pass through the narrows. Dorothy smiled. "See? We're not stupid. Nice to know what we're doing, eh?"

Within a half hour, they were in the Okisollo channel bound for Johnstone Strait. That's when the wind came up fast from the southeast; it was dampened by the nearby land and trees, but strong and steady. The water got choppy, and the rain whipped and splattered on *Destiny*'s windshield. "I've got to slow down," Paul said. "Can't see where we're going." They traveled the next 10 miles at three to four knots, heading to the gray, misty, and darkening light at the end of the channel. The rain, gray sky, and dark green forest on both sides of the channel made it seem as though they were in tunnel. When they got to the entrance to Johnstone Strait, Paul stuck the bow of *Destiny* about 50 meters into the Strait, the waves now at two-to-three feet and the wind increasing—the weather radio said, to 25-30 knots within the next couple of hours, changing to the northwest. *Destiny* bobbed up and down, rocked side to side, and her bow slapped the waves, the wind now at their port stern, making a following sea, then a confused sea, an entirely new situation for Paul. "How far to Chatham Point?"

"About three miles," Dorothy said. "You can barely see the outline up there."

Paul squinted into the rain and slapping windshield wipers. "I see it. We're going in behind there, to the port side, right?"

Dorothy pointed to the drawing in the guidebook. "We get in behind the Point as close to the land as we can. See right there? That's the anchorage in Otter Bay. There will probably be some other boats there."

Paul increased and decreased the throttle, trying to stay ahead of the following sea, but not too far so as to swamp the stern. *Destiny* seemed woozy, unbalanced, and pushed along. Dorothy held on to the seat and his belt. "We should be there in a half hour." The shifting wind rocked *Destiny* side to side. "Anybody getting sick? Ida, you look a little green."

Ida grabbed Paul's brandy and took a couple of swallows out of the bottle. "I'll be fine as soon as we stop."

"There," Dorothy said. "That's the Chatham Point light. Pull into Otter Bay on your port side."

Paul gripped the wheel with white knuckles, turned to port slowly, took some heavy waves on the port beam, rocked, slowed, and drove into the bay, almost to the land. "The depth gauge says twenty-five feet. Shall I go farther?"

"A little more, then we'll turn the bow," Dorothy said. They drifted.

Dorothy turned to Ida. "Could you go out and unhook the anchor chain?"

Ida pulled up the hood on her rain jacket and made her way along the rail to the bow, unhooked the chain fastener, and kicked the anchor loose. She motioned. Dorothy pushed the down arrow on the windlass controller, and the anchor started dropping. The chain went slack. Paul backed up *Destiny* until the anchor grabbed, and Beth snapped on the anchor light as Ida made her way back to the pilothouse. The wind howled as it shifted to the northwest and then slowed in the protected bay; the rain picked up, splattering ceaselessly on the roof as darkness crept over *Destiny*, eerie, like a shroud. They were alone in the bay.

Paul shut down the engine, turned, and took a long pull from his bottle of brandy. He wiped his mouth with the back of his hand and smiled at Dorothy. "Thanks for being my first mate." He nodded at Beth and Ida. "I'm pretty lucky to have such a good crew. Anybody up for a bowl of soup?"

13

It rained all night, all the next day, and until three am the following night. Paul drank and slept, and the girls read navigation and guidebooks. Dorothy took pages of notes, and they carefully studied the route for the next day's journey. Ida memorized the names of all the land features, Beth reckoned the time and distance, and Dorothy studied the tide and current tables. The forecast called for partly cloudy skies and light winds of seven to eight knots from the northwest.

They awakened early. Dorothy started the engine, Ida helped as Dorothy pulled up the anchor with the windlass, Beth made coffee and started breakfast, and by the time Paul woke up, dressed, and went to the head, Dorothy had steered *Destiny* out of Otter Bay and into Johnston Strait. Ominous gray daylight appeared in the east, and *Destiny* settled into a smooth pace at seven knots.

"Good morning," said Dorothy. "Since I'm your first mate, I decided to let you sleep while we got things underway. Everything is shipshape, Captain. Have some coffee."

Paul pushed his hand through his tousled hair. "Are you sure you know what you're doing?"

"Aye, sir. We've got the route figured out for the day, and we should pull into Alert Bay at about two thirty or three. We should have partly cloudy skies and a light breeze from the northwest."

"It's almost seventy miles. We won't get there by then."

Dorothy pointed to her notebook. "Right now, we are at the high flood tide, and it ebbs to the north until about one o'clock. The tide will push us all morning. I'll bet we add three knots to our speed at the same rpm."

Paul tipped his head. "When did you learn all that?"

"We've been studying. We decided if we're going to be a good crew, we need to give you a break. Beth has some bacon and eggs ready. Why don't you have some breakfast?"

Paul shrugged and moved to a stool in the galley. Beth smiled and put a steaming plate of bacon and eggs in front of him. "Would you like some cinnamon toast?"

"Yes, please." Paul ate slowly, silently.

Ida and Dorothy chatted about the landscape and Ida's hope for finding Joel Martin. Dorothy took one hand from the wheel and turned. "What are you going to do when you find him?"

"I've been thinking about that. I'm going to ask him point-blank if Janice Corley is his mother, and then tell him she's my mother too."

"Then what?"

"I guess we'll take it from there, and see what it means for the future. I'm not really sure. I want to get to know Joel, if he'll let me, but we'll have to keep it a secret from my father. Maybe we could see each other a couple of times a year. Maybe he will write letters or send emails."

"It's going to change your life one way or another. You can't go back from this."

Ida nodded. "I'm worried about Danny, my fiancé. He doesn't understand how important this is to me. Our wedding is planned for August, and I don't think he likes the idea of me being away and having another man in my life, even though he's my half brother."

"He'll probably adjust—especially if he loves you."

"Oh, he loves me, and I love him, but he seems, ah, immature."

"You did take off suddenly...and there's the wedding."

"Still, he could be more supportive, don't you think?"

Dorothy laughed. "Is he open to change? I know Paul isn't. He's stubborn as a rock."

Paul climbed up the stairs. "Everything going okay up here, mate?"

"Doing fine. I haven't touched the throttle, and we've speeded up from seven to nine knots." She pointed at the instruments.

"*Destiny* seems to handle it fine, don't you think?"

Dorothy patted the steering wheel. "*Destiny*'s a fine boat. You made a good choice."

Paul raised his eyebrows, leaned his elbows on the dashboard, and watched two eagles soar and dive, each grabbing a fish. Dorothy patted his shoulder. "I'm glad you can relax. Let me know when you want to take the wheel. Wow, look now, we're at ten knots. Seems like the ebb tide is running at a three-knot current."

Destiny made good time through the Strait. Paul woke up from a nap just as Beth carried a plate of sandwiches and fresh coffee up to the pilot-house. Ida was watching the shore and checking the map. Beth handed her a napkin. "There's egg salad or tuna fish. Help yourself."

Beth looked out the windshield. "Where are we?"

Ida pointed behind her and then to her right. "We passed West Thurlow Island back there, and we're just now passing Hardwicke Island." Ida handed Beth the binoculars. "If you look up there on the right, you can see Port Neville. Do we need fuel? We can stop there."

Dorothy checked the gauges. "We'll be fine all the way to Alert Bay. We can get fuel there. The guidebook says Alert Bay fuel is probably cleaner—they sell more."

Beth gasped. "Look, killer whales up ahead. It looks like a whole pod." She handed Ida the binoculars and grabbed her whale identification book. "Let's go up on the flybridge. We can see a lot better."

They slipped on their jackets, took their sandwiches and coffee up the stairs, and settled on to the bench under the canopy. The whales were feeding leisurely. Dorothy slowed the boat as they got closer. Beth showed Ida a page of ID photos from the book. "I can't tell yet, but it looks like it could be the A-one Pod and the A-twelve Matriline. I count six or seven."

Ida leaned forward. "I see seven."

Dorothy slowed *Destiny* to a near idle. The tide had turned, so *Destiny* only made slow headway. The whales moved slowly toward them.

Beth pointed. "See that first one on the right? The dorsal fin is curved like a sword."

Ida looked at the photos. "Could that be Scimitar?"

"Could be. There's a large male too. That's probably her son Nimpkish."

Ida hurried down the stairs, stepped in the cabin, and clasped her hands. Her eyes turned deep green. "Can we shut down the engine? Maybe they'll come closer."

Dorothy shifted to neutral and watched the water. "We're probably moving backward at one knot or so, but we've got plenty of room." She shut off the engine. The only sounds were the lapping waves and the breeze in the flag.

Paul woke up, rubbing his eyes and struggling up the steps. "What happened?"

"Nothing. I shut down the engine. Look out there."

Paul turned, his jaw dropping. "How many are there?"

"There are seven." Ida pointed to the page, handing the book to Beth. Her head rose up and down as she compared photos of dorsal fins and white saddles to the approaching killer whales. "For sure it's the A-one Pod. See those two in front? The first one's Scimitar. She's the grandmother. That big one beside her is Nimpkish, her son, and next to him is Simoom, her daughter. Those are Simoom's offspring behind her. The closest ones are Echo and Stormy, the males; Misty and Eclipse are her daughters."

Paul raised his eyebrows. "You know all that from those pictures?"

"See, each one has a distinctive saddle, that white part by their dorsal fins, and each dorsal fin has identifiable features. It's not hard if you know where to look."

Ida stepped out the door. "They're coming closer."

Everyone moved to the stern deck. Ida put on her life jacket, tied a line around her waist, tied the other end around a cleat, stepped out onto the swim platform, and dropped to her knees. The pod had surrounded *Destiny*, and their breathing sent plumes of mist into the air, splashes of sunlight making rainbows in the droplets of water. They were huge, like sleek black limousines moving around the boat. Nimpkish and Echo nudged *Destiny*, as if playing, and the others dove under *Destiny*, coming up on the other side, and then dove under bow to stern. *Destiny* rocked in the gentle waves made by the whales. Dorothy, Paul, and Beth leaned over the starboard rail, mouths open, breathing rapidly. Ida stayed perfectly still. Scimitar surfaced two meters from the swim platform, her right eye gleaming in the sun. She floated quietly as *Destiny* bobbed up and down. Scimitar stared into Ida's eyes. Her head buzzed like honeybees in a hive.

Ida was no longer in her body, yet the line around her waist dug in, holding her as Scimitar's eye pulled her in, as though she was sucked into a new reality by a whirlwind. Her entire consciousness seemed to take on the shape of Scimitar's eye, and then disappear into deep blackness, seeing years run by as though she was racing through time-lapse photography, seeing herself as a floating spirit in the Milky Way galaxy, as a mature woman, as a pouty teenager, as a silly little girl, and then as a tiny baby with hands folded, a gentle presence waiting to be born. Scimitar blew a misty cloud. Ida inhaled deeply and tasted the salt spray, the cold splashes making her face bright pink. She shook her head, wiping her eyes with one hand, feeling her cheeks and mouth, and held on to *Destiny* with the other.

Scimitar dove, and the pod gathered 20 meters behind the boat and traveled on, their curiosity apparently satisfied.

Ida stood up and came through the transom door to the deck, her hands shaking. She took Beth's arm. "I don't know what just happened, but I felt captured—Scimitar's eye."

"Are you okay?"

"I think so, but I saw some things."

"Are you frightened?"

"No, just blown away. I saw myself as a baby in the Milky Way galaxy. Can you believe it? I was waiting to be born."

"Let's make some tea," Beth said. "Let's keep this to ourselves."

Cups in hand, they made their way up the stairs and into the pilothouse. Dorothy started the engine, and shifted into gear. "We should be in Alert Bay in a couple of hours."

Paul turned to Beth. "Do those killer whales always travel together like that?"

"Yes, the offspring stay with their mother until she dies. Often the males swim beside her and keep her from harm."

"They stay with her all their lives?"

"They protect her, and they help her offspring learn how to find fish."

"They seem so beautiful together, the children with their mother—like a family."

"They've had ten or twelve thousand years to learn how to live together, so they must have figured out something."

Dorothy turned to Paul. "Would you like to take the helm for a while?"

Paul nodded his head, wiping his eyes with the back of his sleeve. "Just give me a minute."

14

"Alert Bay Harbormaster, this is *Destiny*, *Destiny*, *Destiny*."

"Go ahead, *Destiny*. This is Alert Bay Harbormaster."

"I'm a forty-two-foot power boat looking for overnight moorage. Do you have anything available?" Paul asked.

"*Destiny*, you're in luck. I have a space on the main dock. You can head in, come clear to the end, just ahead of the sixty-five-foot seiner. It's a starboard tie."

"Okay, we're about two kilometers out. See you in thirty minutes. *Destiny* out."

Paul motioned to Ida. "You girls put the fenders down on the starboard side and get the lines ready."

Dorothy took the wine bottle off the dashboard table. "It's only two o'clock. At least you can wait until five."

"You're right. Don't need the Coast Guard snooping around again."

Dorothy stepped outside the cabin and poured the wine into the water and then stuck the empty bottle into the trash.

Paul hurried down the stairs, put on a windbreaker, and climbed the stairs to the flybridge. "I'm going to drive from up here. Can you come up and keep a lookout?"

Dorothy joined him on the flybridge, and Ida handed a rolled-up line to Beth. "Here's the long one for the bow. I'll take the stern."

Ida motioned at the flybridge. "I'm worried. They'll be lucky to make it around the island. Is there anything we can do?"

"No. They have a classic alcoholic relationship. That has to end before they can get better—either he quits drinking or she quits trying to control him. They're too enmeshed."

"Tough stuff. At least it's better now with Dorothy knowing how to drive. I'm sorry to leave them, but I want to be out of here by five o'clock and on our way to Joel Martin's boat."

"Let's hope we can find a water taxi. It'll be light for another six hours."

Paul slowed *Destiny* as he moved into the harbor and along the main dock. He nosed in ahead of the fishing boat and revved up the stern thruster, pulling the stern toward the dock. Beth and Ida tossed lines to a couple of guys on the dock. They tied up without incident, and Dorothy jumped off with the power cord. "The plug is behind you, past the seiner. You'll need your extension cord."

Beth handed Dorothy another cord. She unrolled it and plugged it in.

"I've got shore power," Paul said, shutting down the engine.

The Harbormaster waved at Paul. "Welcome to Alert Bay."

Ida stepped off the boat into the bright sunlight. She wore green shorts and a tight white T- shirt. Her hair was tied back in a ponytail through a white baseball cap. She smiled and put her hands on her hips. "Is there a water taxi nearby?" Three men gawked.

One man moved forward. "I've got a water taxi," he said. "Where do you need to go?"

Ida pulled a folded map out of her back pocket. "We need to go over here by the Orca Labs. I need to find Joel Martin and his research boat. I think it's called *Spyhopper*." Beth pulled their roller bags over to the side of the boat. She pointed to the boat behind them. "Our customs' friend said it is an old fishing boat probably like that one."

"I know the boat—*Spyhopper*—they've been in here for groceries and laundry. Likely they're anchored out there by Blackney Pass, probably in Parson Bay, about twenty-five kilometers or so. We can head over that way and raise them on the radio. When do you want to go?"

"Right now. How long will it take?"

"The weather's good—we'll be moving against the tide—probably less than two hours." He looked at the bags. "Are you staying overnight?"

Ida looked at Beth and then shrugged her shoulders. "I guess it depends on what happens when we get there."

"I can hang around," he said. "If you're only there for a couple of hours, we can still be back before dark. I'll have to charge you sixty-five dollars each way."

Paul came down the stairs from the flybridge. His face was red. "I'm sorry to see you go. Thanks for the help."

Dorothy rushed over and held Beth's hands. "Thank you both so much." Her chin quivered as her eyes got teary. "I'm not sure I know what to do—you know, by ourselves."

"Lower your expectations," Beth said. "Like we've discussed, slow down your trip. Travel only in the mornings. You've learned to handle *Destiny* like an old hand. Maybe you can hire a guide when you get to Port Hardy."

Dorothy let her head slump. "I'm going to check with my sister. Maybe we can stay with her for a while. I'll cope. I always have. Let's stay in touch."

"Sure. I've got your cell phone number."

Ida kissed Dorothy on the cheek, grabbed both roller bags, and turned to the water taxi captain. "Let's go."

The captain helped them get on board and stow their bags. He handed Ida and Beth life jackets and helped them to their seats. The taxi was a pilothouse aluminum boat, and the seats were covered with vinyl, like a bus. He started the engine. "This is a twenty-nine-foot Eagle Craft." He smiled. "The engine is a Volvo D-six, three hundred and sixty horsepower. Very safe. Very fast." He slipped the lines off the cleats on the dock, backed up, turned, and headed out into the harbor. Soon they were clipping along over choppy water, the boat's bow slapping the waves, spraying up on the windows. Ida and Beth held on to the rail on the seat in front of them, Ida's pony tail flopping up and down. She tucked her arms in to hold her breasts from bouncing.

"Can you see where you're going?" Ida shouted.

"Just relax, there's nothing to worry about. I'll go down Johnstone Strait and through Blackney Pass. Keep your eyes open for killer whales. There should be some around."

She turned to Beth. "A week ago I had given up finding him, and here we are, just an hour away. I'm scared."

Beth nodded her head and smiled. "I'm not even part of this, and I'm a little scared too. What are you going to say?"

Ida tilted her head. "I think I'll say my name is Ida and we have the same mother. Is that too bold?"

"Maybe you'd better ask him. You're still not certain, right?"

Ida shook her head. They bounced along for nearly an hour when she heard the radio crackle. "*Spyhopper, Spyhopper, Spyhopper*, this is the water taxi *Eagle Eye*. Do you copy?" There was no response. He tried again. "They're probably behind the island. We'll try again when we get up to the west end of Parsons."

"Ida, look over there—killer whales, maybe a dozen of them."

Ida shaded her eyes. A pod was traveling easterly through Blackney, diving and surfacing, moving quickly. "They're feeding," the captain said, slowing down. "The salmon run through here."

He tried the radio again. "Yes, this is *Spyhopper*. I read you *Eagle Eye*. What's going on out there?"

"I've got a couple of women passengers. Say they need to see Joel Martin. Where are you anchored?"

"You've got Troy here. Why do they need to see Joel?"

"Don't know. Are you tucked in a cove somewhere?"

"We're about halfway down Parson's Cove. Is there a problem?"

The captain looked at Ida. She shook her head back and forth. "Just need to see him. No problems."

"The nice lady says she just needs to see him."

"I'll get Joel. We'll watch for you *Eagle Eye*. *Spyhopper* out."

The captain dropped down to two-to-three knots as they saw *Spyhopper* in a small cove near the shore. He pulled up slowly and tossed a line. Troy tied off the line and watched as Ida and Beth stepped out of the door. Hazel, and Jean were standing nearby, and Joel walked up to the group. "Who needs to see Joel Martin?"

"I do," Ida said. "Can we come aboard?"

Joel glanced at Troy and shrugged his shoulders and smiled.

"Sure. Jean, could you please warm up some coffee?"

Troy lowered a platform tied by ropes. Ida and Beth climbed out onto the platform, waves rocking the taxi, and then Hazel helped them up onto the deck. "I'm Hazel Chartrand, Joel and Jean's graduate student."

"Hello. I'm Ida Corley, and this is Beth Odem."

Troy mumbled, "Troy Campbell. I take care of *Spyhopper*."

The captain shut down the engine of the water taxi. "We'll hang here for a while."

"I'll get you some coffee," Joel said. Then he turned to Ida. "Come on in the galley and sit down. Then you can tell me what this is all about."

Ida sat down, Beth slid in beside her, Hazel stepped away, and Jean poured coffee. "Milk or sugar?"

"Both please," Ida said. She stirred her coffee and then blurted out, "I am Ida May Corley, from Albuquerque, New Mexico, and Janice Corley was my mother. Is she your mother too?"

"What? I don't know anyone from Albuquerque."

"I saw an old letter from my mother that said she had a son. I found your name on the sign-in book for Mom's funeral. Was she your mother? Was Fred your father?"

"Fred who?"

"I don't know, just Fred. Are you my half brother?"

Joel shook his head. "There are a lot of Martins in the world. I'm not the one you're looking for."

"The sign-in said Joel Martin from Victoria."

"Martin is a common name. You shouldn't have come all this way. I'm a professor at UBC—you should've called me there."

"I tried." Ida sipped her coffee as tears filled her eyes. "Can I ask you something? When is your birthday?"

Joel turned his palms up. "I was born in May, 1956. I was forty-eight this year."

Ida closed her eyes and inhaled through her teeth. "You're three years too old." She dropped her head into her hands, shaking. Beth put her hand on Ida's shoulder, glancing at Joel. "It's been a long trip. This is a huge disappointment."

"Three years too old?"

Ida wiped her eyes with her sleeve. "Yes, too old. Mom's baby boy was born in 1959, in Victoria I think." Ida motioned out the galley door. "You'd better tell the water taxi captain we'll be along soon."

Beth talked with the captain and then came back. The galley was quiet. Jean cut up red peppers and squash as she watched Ida. Joel clasped his hands behind his head. "We can offer you dinner, and the water taxi skipper, too. There's plenty for everyone."

Ida looked at Beth, who nodded. "Thank you. We're both worn out."

Joel stood up and turned to Jean. She smiled and nodded. "Let's get another salmon out of the cooler. Looks like we have guests for dinner." Joel motioned for Troy. "Are you still going to Alert Bay in the morning?"

"Going to take the small Zodiac. Need parts for the outboard. Jean wants me to pick up mail and groceries—fresh fruit."

Joel turned back to Ida. "Why don't you and Beth stay for dinner and then stay the night. Troy can take you back in the morning. You need rest."

Jean raised her head. "Beth, you can share the back cabin with me, and Ida can bunk with Hazel."

"Sounds like we're imposing," Ida said.

"No problem. You'd have to leave right now if you want to get back before dark. Go ahead and pay the captain so he can get back. It's not an imposition, right, Jean?"

Jean offered a smile. "Always room for two more."

Hazel showed Ida and Beth around *Spyhopper* and explained how to use the head and the shower. "You have to pump salt water up into the toilet to flush it. The shower and sink are fresh water, but please use them sparingly." Ida and Beth washed their faces, changed clothes, and followed Hazel as she showed them the research equipment arranged neatly along the port side under the roof deck and surrounded by heavy plastic curtains—laptop computers, cameras, listening devices, recorders, and waterproof boxes full of notes and CDs. Everything was under double plastic covers, shielded against the wind and rain, tucked away alongside folding tables.

Joel came down from the pilothouse. "Radio says could have some weather, but not until tomorrow night. Everyone like barbeque? It's great on salmon." He and Troy set up a propane-fired grill out on deck and turned on the heat. Jean brought a plate of salmon.

Hazel and Troy set up a couple of folding tables and chairs, spread out a tablecloth, and set the table with heavy porcelain plates. Everyone sat down to a dinner of barbequed salmon, sautéed peppers and squash, and leafy romaine lettuce salad. Jean brought out fresh coffee and strawberry pie for dessert. Salt air sharpened the taste of everything.

Joel stood up. "Make yourselves comfortable. I've got to listen to some recordings."

"Recordings?" Beth asked.

"My research. Like Ida, I'm searching for something. For me it's a unique sound, maybe a squeak or a whistle. Actually, it's quite simple. I need to find a new word—trouble is it's a killer whale word, and so far it's unfathomable."

"That's your research? Looking for a whale word?"

"Sounds silly, right? Here, let me show you." Joel nodded at Troy. "Okay, let's play some whale chatter."

Troy snapped on a CD player. Quiet recordings of whale clicks and songs filled the boat with surround sound. Troy took a plastic baggie out of his pocket, rolled a joint, and took a deep drag. He passed it around. Beth smiled, shrugged her shoulders, and sucked in a big hit. It passed to Hazel, and then Joel. He held it out to Ida. "I'm sorry for your disappointment. This will help you sleep."

Ida paused for a moment and took the joint. Danny would be furious with her if he knew. She inhaled deeply, coughed, and then inhaled again, holding her breath, wishing this time in her life would quickly float on by. *Sonofabitch*, as her brother would say. *This is a wild goose chase.* Danny was right...rational Danny, practical Danny, dog whisperer Danny. Sonofabitch. But Mike? What the hell was going on around here? The lights turned fuzzy.

Troy rolled another joint, passed it around, and Ida slowly ate her strawberry pie, staring at the crust, imagining the flour, the oil, and Jean's rolling pin—"You pinched the edges, right?"

Jean smiled. "I did, and I'd do it again."

"My mother always pinched the edges." She wiped her mouth, put down her fork, raised her chin, and looked at Joel's face, his gray eyes locking onto her green eyes. She didn't blink as she welled up. She wiped her eyes with a napkin. "Do you think everything happens for a reason?"

"Say again?"

"Well, you're a scientist. I was wondering if you think there's a reason behind everything that happens."

"Well, actually, I think it's a lot more complicated than that. Sometimes events cause other events, you know, a clear chain of events. The motor turns the prop, the prop displaces water, and the boat moves. Other times, I think, events happen in proximity to each other, but there's no observable causal connection; it's hard to pin down a reason why they occurred together in space and time. Most scientists don't like to admit it, but we live with a lot of serendipity. So, the short answer is that sometimes there are clear reasons, and other times events are just synchronous. They happen at the same time, often in the same space, but you can't find a cause."

Ida took a deep breath and looked around, meeting eyes, one person at a time, except for Troy. He was gazing out at the darkening horizon. She folded her hands. "Please don't laugh at me, but a killer whale led me to you. I was about to give up when Mike told me to go north."

Joel cocked his head. Hazel and Jean leaned in.

"He *told* you? How's that?"

"Mike came up to our kayak with his mother and his sister—Slick and Alki. They were really close, like right there." Ida pointed at the end of the table. "I was scared."

"Jay twenty-six," Beth said. "Near Victoria, just off Sidney Island."

Joel raised his eyebrows and smiled at Beth. "You understand pods and numbers?"

"I've worked on a whale-watching boat out of Victoria, so I know the southern residents. Mike usually travels with his mother and sister. He's easy to spot with his tall dorsal fin." Beth looked down and grinned. "Ida had a major encounter with Mike when she was on a tour. I've never seen anything like it."

"An encounter? What do you mean?"

"I mean when Ida and Mike first met—their first date. It was later when we saw them from the kayak." Beth smiled at Ida, who shrugged her shoulders, and then Beth looked back at Joel. She put her hand up to her mouth to cover her uncontained laughter. "Mike swam right up to the boat, rolled over, and waved his penis at Ida, I mean right at her, like 'Hey, pretty lady, check this out.' Then he gave her the eye—the killer whale eye."

Joel laughed, and Troy raised his eyebrows. "Are you sure?"

Beth shook her head. "Yes, I'm sure. I'd say I can recognize a penis when I see one—especially a five-footer." Her face reddened as she turned to Ida, who had her face in her hands, shaking with laughter. "You think that's something," Ida said. "I'm a nurse, and I can recognize little ones, big ones, and everything in between—doesn't take a rocket scientist."

Joel slapped his thigh, laughing uncontrollably, putting his hand on Beth's arm. Jean stepped in between Joel and Beth, turning to Ida, Jean's eyebrows furrowed, intense. "What did you hear in the kayak? What did the killer whale say?"

"It really wasn't a sound," Ida said. "My whole mind filled up with a command—*go north*. Made me quiver all over."

"Was there any sound at all?"

"Maybe some chirps, like a baby bird. When he swam away, I swear I could feel his feelings skipping over the water and into me—warm, shivery feelings. Call me crazy if you want, but things like that don't just happen, do they? Mike came to me for some reason, don't you think?" She put her open palm on her heart. She looked out at the horizon, but all she could see was black, shimmering water, tiny skips of light from a rising one-quarter moon. She was light as a feather, floating between the stares from Joel and Jean, Joel earnest, focused, like a teacher, and Jean with her arms folded, looking skeptical.

"It's more subtle—hard to explain, like maybe you're thinking of your friend, Beth, and just then she calls your cell phone. Maybe you have a dream about a boyfriend at an amusement park, and the next day he calls and tells you he had fun at an amusement park. Or, I remember one time in June when I was talking with Jean about Orcas spyhopping." He smiled at Jean. She squeezed his hand. "Remember? I had told you I hope you get to see it up close. We were doing about four knots when, just then, a young male and his mother spyhopped abut twenty meters ahead of us. We almost jumped out of our skin. Now, I'd say those events are synchronous—they happened together, and it's as if they knew, but there's no clear reason—certainly nothing I can figure."

Jean tipped her head back and spoke slowly. "True scientists call that a coincidence. It doesn't mean anything. We tend to find meaning in things and to project our wishes onto the world."

Ida turned to Joel. "Do killer whales see things we can't see?"

"Perhaps. I happen to believe we can communicate with them." He looked at Jean, who was scowling. "I'm convinced we have interspecies communication. Whales can take you places with their eyes and their songs. I've had experiences with them, or I should say one. I entered into her mind through her eye. She was in the Vancouver aquarium—Bjossa was her name."

Ida clasped her hands together. "That happened to me with Scimitar's eye, back there in the Johnstone Strait. A whole pod came up to our boat. I promise you I'm not crazy. In her eye I saw myself as a baby in the Milky Way galaxy."

"A close encounter with a killer whale can be disorienting," Jean said. "They are huge, and when their eye is visible, it can be overwhelming. People often hallucinate or have hypnagogic images when they are overwhelmed."

"It's more than that," Joel said. "A whole lot more."

Jean smiled and looked at Ida. "Now you know why I'm here with Joel. He's got to have a hard scientist around or he loses all credibility."

"Hey, come on. My articles on killer whale echolocation and communication are great studies."

"Granted, but your work with interspecies communication and LSD hurt your reputation."

He dismissed Jean with a wave and turned to Ida. "Some say it's a main doorway. If you let them lock eyes with you—one of theirs with both of yours—they can transport you, if only for a few seconds, and you can see things. Ask Hazel. Kwakiutl elders tell stories about it. Right, Hazel? A whale's eye can capture you, take you on a journey."

Hazel opened her eyes and touched her breast above her heart. "Our elders say killer whales have many things to teach us, but we have to be open."

Ida leaned forward and locked eyes with Hazel. "What kind of things?"

"Mostly about our journey through the web of life, how all living things are deeply connected, how to live in a never-ending family. They've learned how to exist peacefully. There's a special knowing, extrasensory. Some people call it spiritual intuition, or telepathy. My grandfather called it heart knowing."

Ida thought back to the day she met Mike, when he looked at her, then later, in the gloaming, when Mike told her in her mind to go north. She shivered, and because she just then got goose bumps; because Troy, and Hazel were all nodding their heads slowly and their eyes were heavy-lidded from marijuana and the sounds of whale songs; because she felt steady and balanced even on a rocking boat, and because Joel was looking at her gently, not with desire, but with eyes of a longtime friend—a surge of warmth rippled through her, and she breathed deeply as a strange light flickered before her eyes. Next time, unafraid, she would let the whale's eye take her there. She could not stop grinning. "I'm getting tired. Where did you say I would sleep?"

Joel nodded to Hazel; she stood and led Ida to her cabin in the back, and Jean helped Beth roll her suitcase to her adjacent cabin. "Use that little table to unpack your bag, and there are empty drawers under the bed."

"I'll just unpack a few things."

"If you don't mind, I have a few things to say."

"Sure," said Beth, sitting down on the bed.

"I saw how Joel was looking at you, and you didn't mind his attention, right?"

"I didn't notice anything unusual. Seemed like he was just being nice."

"He's quite attractive, don't you think?"

"Yes. He seems healthy and fit."

"I don't want you to get any ideas. Joel and I have been teaching colleagues at UBC for years. We're research associates, but we are also longtime lovers. He's essentially spoken for."

Beth turned her palms up. "I haven't even thought about it. He's simply a gracious host and an interesting scientist."

"Did you really have to talk about the whale penis? Sure did make him laugh. Sort of an odd remark. Were you flirting with Joel?"

"No, it was the truth. It was very odd, and he's a whale researcher. Don't you think that was unusual?"

"Well, I guess so, but killer whales are often playful and have erections. We've been lovers for years, and I think this will be the summer when we finally let people know. He treats me like a colleague in front of other people, but we both know what goes on underneath." Jean ran her fingers through her hair and smiled. "*Spyhopper* is a small boat, and having Hazel around in all manner of dress has him a little bit flustered. I noticed you're not wearing a ring. Do you have a boyfriend in your life?"

"My husband died of cancer not long ago, and I'm taking some time off from work. I'm a social worker from Vancouver, and for many years we were here on the island."

"Sorry. I didn't mean to sound harsh. You are a very nice-looking woman and I could tell Joel was intrigued. Sorry. I guess I feel a little threatened."

"Please," Beth said. "I have no interest, and we're leaving in the morning."

"Now I'm embarrassed. I shouldn't have said anything, but he is my man, and I've got to keep an eye on him. You know those whales are free spirited. The males from one pod visit females other pods when they're breeding, and sometimes they have sex with different females just for fun. It's the way they are. They don't mean anything by it. Joel admires them."

Beth nodded. "I guess I'll go in the washroom and get ready for bed."

"Sure. Take your time. Please don't let the water run while you brush your teeth. Fresh water is a real commodity around here."

Jean snored intermittently all night. Just as Beth fell asleep, she would be awakened by a loud snort and five minutes of steady snoring. She twisted the ends of her socks to make earplugs, and covered her head with the blanket and pillow, but Jean's snoring could not be silenced. Beth thought it would be inappropriate to awaken her, especially since she was a guest, but by morning, she could have smacked her with a shoe. As the gray light of dawn came through the porthole, Beth got dressed and went to the washroom. She moved out to a chair under the roof deck and wrapped herself in a blanket. The rain began, and soon was a steady downpour. They would not be going anywhere today, certainly not in an open Zodiac.

15

eth dozed and then smelled coffee and bacon. Jean was in the galley making breakfast. Hazel emerged from her cabin in a heavy sweater, Joel came down the stairs from the pilothouse in a yellow rain jacket, and Ida sat down in the galley dressed in a dark blue sweater and a wool watch cap, eyes swollen, chewing on her fingernails. Troy parted the heavy plastic curtain and stepped inside, shaking water off his yellow slicker as he hung it on a hook. He slipped out of his suspenders and pulled down his rain pants. He was dressed in faded green sweats. Joel glanced at Troy. "Everything tied down out there?"

Troy looked down. "Covers on the Zodiacs needed to be fixed. Anchor's holding, but we've swung closer to shore."

"Looks like we're socked in for a while."

"It'll rain all day."

"Maybe longer."

"How much rain do you get around here?" Ida asked.

Troy rubbed his chin. "Twelve or thirteen days of rain in July—maybe two or three inches, not like November—twenty-two days of rain."

"Breakfast," Jean shouted.

Everyone gathered around the table. Joel slid in the booth next to Beth. "You look tired. Did you sleep well?"

"Not really. I was restless most of the night."

"Were you comfortable in that bed?"

Beth crossed her arms, hugging herself. "Yes, the rocking is comforting."

Joel laughed. "This old round bottom boat rolls a lot, especially with the wind we had. Even in this cove, the waves were one to two feet. I've gotten used to it. The rolling puts me to sleep."

Jean slid a plate in front of Joel—eggs, bacon, and a couple of bran muffins. "Time to eat."

Joel glanced at Jean. She had her hands on her hips.

"We'll try to get you bundled up for a nap today," Joel said. "Sleeping on a cold, rainy afternoon is good for the soul."

Beth reminded herself to search in both heads for some earplugs. Maybe she could find a tactful way to ask Joel. He must know that Jean snored like a trumpet.

After breakfast, Joel ushered Beth into an easy chair tucked in a corner by a bookcase. He leaned down so their cheeks nearly touched and pushed a lever that raised a footrest and tipped the chair back. He spoke quietly in her ear. "You can rest here. Help yourself to the books, and don't worry, nobody will bother you." He looked into Beth's eyes and grinned.

Jean pushed Joel aside and handed Beth a mug of tea. "Drink it while it's hot—it'll keep you warm."

They spent the day reading, cleaning, playing Scrabble, poring over navigation charts, and listening to whale sounds. After a lunch of cold cuts and salad, Troy passed around a pipe. It wasn't long before everyone was stoned except Jean. She sat in the galley with her arms crossed as Hazel sat down across the table. "I read your eagle wildlife guide. It's quite informative."

"Thank you. I wanted to write something that would be useful."

"Did you take the photographs yourself?"

"Most of them. The close-ups are stock photos, some from wildlife photographers. I've seen a lot of things no one has photographed."

"Me too, and my grandfather has told me stories about bald eagles—they're magical, like killer whales."

"Do you study them?"

"Not like you, but I've known the sound of eagles and watched them soar ever since I was a little girl. Sometimes I'd pretend I was flying along with them."

The corners of Jean's mouth turned up. "I imagine that too."

Hazel smiled gently and extended her hand with the pipe. "Want to try a little?"

"I'd better not."

"You know it'll help you relax."

Jean leaned toward Hazel. "I worry when I smoke."

"About what?"

"I don't want to lose control. I mean what if I say something?"

"You won't. You have a good heart. You might laugh a little or loosen up, but you won't say anything you'll be sorry for. Those things are not in you."

Jean got up and pulled the galley curtain closed. She took the pipe and inhaled, coughing slightly. She looked around. "I don't feel anything."

"Take another drag and hold it in."

Jean inhaled again, held her breath, and let it out slowly. "If I was an eagle, I could sit on an egg for hours."

"For hours?" Hazel tilted her head.

"Sure. I could settle right down in a warm nest on an egg and be very peaceful." Jean rubbed her breasts gently. "My down is very soft and my soft is very down." She opened her eyes wide. "What did I just say?"

"It's fine," Hazel said. "You're just imagining what it's like to feel like an eagle. I wouldn't mind sitting on an egg myself." She put her hand up to her mouth to stifle a giggle, then she and Jean both started chuckling.

"Have you seen them do acrobatics?" Hazel asked.

"Oh, my yes. It's beautiful. They start high up on a thermal. The male flies under the female and they lock talons, and then they come down tumbling, fumbling." Jean touched her mouth. "I mean they tumble and roll until they almost hit the water. It's a mating ritual. Looks like fun, don't you think?"

"I often wish I could fly like that with a lover."

Jean frowned. "I've noticed you checking out Joel now and then. You understand he's my man, don't you?"

Hazel giggled. "Whatever, but you shouldn't worry about that. My hips are too wide and my breasts are too big. He seems more attracted to slender women, like you. Besides, he's almost twenty years older than me."

"We've been colleagues and research associates for years. We're just waiting for the right time to announce we're, you know, together and soon to be married."

"I see. Once, when I was little, my grandfather and I watched an eagle soar up so high he disappeared. I asked my grandfather where he went, and he said the eagle was a seer, and he has gone to see what the future will bring."

"I've not heard that. I know the eagle is a seer in Kwakiutl mythology, but not that eagles can see the future. How could they ever communicate that?"

"Grandfather said that when he returns, the eagle gathers up others and tells them what will happen to us. Then, if they play—catch sticks, things like that—then we will have good health, love, and fortune. If they pester ospreys and take away their food, it means we will have conflict. And if they attack muskrats or sea otters, it means harm is coming over the horizon."

"We saw those eagles playing catch with that herring—or Troy thought an anchovy. Could one of those eagles be a seer?"

"Grandfather says they're all seers after they have a dozen years. There's something about twelve, but I can't remember."

"What do you like the best about my field guide?"

"I like your writing. It sounds like you care a lot for eagles—there's a kinship."

Jean put both hands on her heart. "I love them, but I can't tell scientists that. Joel loves Orcas, but he can't say so, at least not in scientific journals. We have that in common. I love eagles and he loves whales. You know eagles mate for life, don't you?"

"Yes, but those Orcas don't. With all the males hanging out with their mother and sisters, there'd be too much incest. They need those frisky young males to come from other pods and spread the genes around."

"I know." Jean lowered her voice. "Joel admires those males. I think he wants to be like them."

"I know a lot of males like that."

Jean stood up. "Let's bake some chocolate chip cookies. They would be good for a rainy afternoon, don't you think?"

"Sure." Hazel put the pipe in her pocket. "I'll help make the dough."

"Thank you," Jean said. "You've been very nice—not like many of my students."

Out by the large table, Ida was swaying and listening to the whale sounds from the speakers. Joel sat across the table, eyes closed. A large wave slapped the boat, and Joel raised his head, opening his eyes. "Are you doing okay?"

Ida smiled and then began crying. "What am I going to do now? How will I find him?"

"Things will be okay," Joel said. "You should pick up your life where you left off. Go back to work, relax."

"That's easy for you to say, but things are not the same. My mother had a baby, and I need to find him. I guess I'll go through her things again. Maybe something will turn up."

"Sometimes it's best just to let things be."

Hazel stood up with a sleepy grin on her face, hugged herself, and began rocking and singing quietly. "And when the night is cloudy, there is still a light that shines on me. Shine until tomorrow, let it be. Let it be, let it be, let it be, yeah, let it be. There will be an answer, let it be."

Troy nodded. The steady rainfall seemed to keep time to the music.

In the morning, Troy helped Ida and Beth put their bags in the Zodiac and put on life jackets. They each had a seat, and Troy sat in back, rain hat pulled down over his eyes. Joel leaned over the rail. "You've got my mailing addresses in Alert Bay and in Vancouver. Be sure and let me know how things go." He grinned at Beth. "You're not that far away. I get to Victoria now and then. Should I call you?"

Beth raised her eyebrows in surprise. "Sure. That would be great."

She had rested well. Late last night Joel had handed her a little box of foam earplugs. "Sometimes we can hear Jean all over the boat, like a foghorn."

Troy started the outboard, and they headed out around Parson Island. Clouds were gathering from the north, and the wind whipped up as the Zodiac headed into Blackfish Sound.

Troy raised his hand and pointed. "That's Malcolm Island in the distance and the Plumper Islands on your left." The light Zodiac began slapping on the waves. The tide was ebbing at about two knots, and the wind was from the southeast, gusting to 15 knots.

The motor chugged and stopped. "Damn fuel pump," Troy said. He fussed with the fuel line. "I think we got some bad gas too. Probably some water in it."

He cranked the engine. It sputtered and started, but wouldn't rev up. It ran at just over an idle, enough that they made headway. He shrugged and held up his hands. "I guess that's all it can do. May take us awhile with the current."

Beth took Ida's shaking hand. "I'm sure Troy has a lot of experience. We'll be fine."

Ida shaded her eyes with her hand and gazed over Troy's head to the northwest at an oncoming bank of gray clouds. The wind shifted, swirled, and came at them from the northwest against the ebbing tide, making choppy waves, splashing spray over the side of the Zodiac. Troy cursed under his breath and tried his radio. No response. The bank of clouds puffed, thickened, and suddenly rolled over them with a dense fog. Ida pulled her windbreaker tight, flipped up the hood, and hunkered down. "What's happening? We can't see a thing."

Troy slipped on his life jacket, pulling his blue wool cap down over his ears. He tapped on the broken glass of a compass mounted by the radio, the needle spinning uselessly. "This is not good," he said. "Better sit down on the deck." He tied a rope around his waist and to a loop on the side. He handed a rope to Ida. "Tie that to your life jacket, run it through a loop, and tie the other end to Beth. Keep it loose. If we get tipped over, hold on to the line and stay close to the boat."

"Tipped over?" Beth said. "That water is fifty degrees. We wouldn't last twenty minutes."

"Don't screw up," Ida shouted.

Troy tried the radio again. No response.

The steady flap, flap of the Zodiac against the waves was muffled by the dense, cool fog. They could barely see each other on the boat. "Any idea where we are?" Ida asked.

"We're somewhere in Blackfish Sound."

As quick as it had shifted, the wind became a breeze, and the surface of the water began to calm. Ida took a breath. "What's happening?"

"Wind's calming. The fog will get thicker." Troy checked the top of the orange gas can.

"Have we got enough gas?"

"If we go straight there, we have enough."

"But we don't know where we are."

Troy looked around. Thick fog everywhere. He shut down the engine.

Ida held both of Beth's hands. "We could die," she whispered, biting her lip. It was too soon; there was so much left; Danny was waiting; no idea about Mom's baby; her little dog ER; the empty place in her mind that rattled with dead memories of men; and the idea that maybe, just maybe, she could find a way to be comfortable, freed from feeling so ragged, so unfinished, so afraid. Why did she have to be sexy and desired to feel alive? Would she ever know? Even now, wrapped in dark fog and afraid for her life, she imagined herself dancing through Joel's mind, replacing his glances at Jean and Hazel with fantasies about her—her breasts, her lips, her arms around him. She stood up, put her hands on her ears, and screamed into the air, the sound muffled as though under water, high pitches softened by the misty fog and silence. She plopped down on the seat and buried her head in her hands, Beth rubbing her back. The water moved slowly, and Troy watched the boat drift. "Are you freaking out?"

"No."

"Good. We're not dead, just lost."

Ida shouted at Troy through the fog. "Hey, I'm scared. Aren't you scared?"

"I'm mostly pissed off. The current is to the northwest, so that's the way we're drifting." He pointed behind them. "That's the way we want to go, southwest."

"What can we do?" Ida touched the paddle lashed to the side. "Can we paddle?"

He looked at his watch—11 am. "Paddle if you want, but it won't do any good. If we wait an hour or so, the tide will turn, and the current might help us drift to a better place."

"A better place?"

"Hey, if I burn up gas fighting this current, we could end up out in the Queen Charlotte Strait with no gas at all. No one would ever find us— except the sharks. If we wait for a while, at least the tide could carry us back toward land."

"Do we have any food or water?" Beth asked.

"I've got a couple of Power Bars, and there's three bottles of water under your seat."

"I'm freezing. We're going to die out here, right?"

Troy looked up at the gray sky. "Well, like I said, we're lost. Waiting is our only choice. I don't plan on dying. Don't panic."

Ida hunched her shoulders, squinting at Troy to see his expression. His angular face turned, and in profile, and she saw his smooth, rounded nose and his pointed chin. Just then, he reminded her of her brother, Jeff. His mouth looked like Junior's. She took a deep breath, putting her hands on her cheeks. "I don't want to die, but this is bad. We could die out here, right?"

"I guess we could."

"We're lost in the ocean for Christ's sake."

"All we need is a little light through the fog, just enough to see land. Let's just wait."

"What else can we do?"

"Nothing."

Ida huddled down in her rain jacket, Beth leaned against her side, and Troy pulled his blue wool watch cap down over his ears. They rocked in the waves. They waited.

"I'm not going to die," Ida whispered. "But just in case we do, would you tell me something?"

Troy raised his head. "Tell you what?"

"Tell me if you knew my mother, Janice Corley."

Troy looked away.

"Well, did you know her? We could die out here. What could it matter? Goddamn it, tell me."

"How would I know her?"

"I don't know. I've come so far. You look like my brother. I thought, maybe..."

"Maybe your brother looks like me. How about that?"

Ida dropped her head as Beth wrapped her arms around her.

Suddenly, the boat rocked. Troy grabbed a paddle, stood up, and whacked the seat. "That bitch. I'm glad she's dead."

"Glad she's dead?"

"Yes, I'm fucking glad."

"Was that you at her funeral?"

Troy nodded, sitting back down. "I wanted to make sure she died."

"You used Joel's name?"

Troy turned his head and gazed into the fog.

"So, Janice Corley was your mother too?"

"You've had a good life in Albuquerque—you and your brothers. You know where I lived?

A fucking orphanage."

"So is Fred your father?"

"Hell, I don't know. I guess so. That's what Joel says."

"Joel?"

"We were in the orphanage together."

"I knew it." Ida grabbed Beth by the shoulder.

"Joel watched out for me."

"In Victoria?"

"Yes, the BC Protestant Orphans' Home—just called it the Home."

"Your whole childhood?"

"I was there until I was twelve, and then with different foster parents, but nothing ever worked out. I got a job on a fishing boat for a while when I was sixteen. Came back and worked for the Home. They hired me as staff, helped me finish school."

A puff of breeze swirled and thickened the fog. Ida leaned toward Troy, knees on the deck. "Where's Fred?"

"Probably still in Albuquerque. Joel says he's in a home—old age."

"How does he know?"

"Her letters."

"Letters?"

"Janice wrote letters and sent money to the Home. It was a church charity."

"She knew you were there?"

"I guess. That's why she sent guilt money."

"Guilt money?"

"Yeah, guilt money. She had years to come and get me. Sent money instead."

"She knew where you were?"

"Who knows, but why in the hell would a church in Albuquerque send money to an orphanage in Victoria?"

"Yeah, maybe she knew. You could've said something at the funeral."

"I watched you and your brothers and your father walk out of the church."

"You watched us?"

"That's the life I could've had—walked right by."

"Maybe you didn't miss much." Ida dropped her head.

"I'm glad she's dead. Guess I wasn't good enough. Tossed me aside and kept you."

Quiet gathered around them as Ida stopped talking. She chewed on a thumbnail as she welled up, uncomfortable as her stomach twisted up, making it hard to breathe. She tipped her head back for a moment. "Why haven't I ever known? Why was she hiding it?"

"Probably thought she was protecting you—maybe from me. I was a stain on your family."

"That had to be hard on her too."

"I guess it would be hard if you can't wipe away a stain."

Ida settled down low near the seat. Beth hugged her and began humming as they rocked from side to side, shivering from the cold and the huge truth that closed in around them, pressing in, like the fog.

"Isn't there anything we can do? I hate doing nothing," Beth said.

Troy leaned forward. "Can you sing?"

Beth raised her head. "Sing what?"

"Oh, I don't know, anything with a beat. Something resonant, faster than the waves. Maybe a boat will come by and hear us."

"How likely is that?"

Troy shrugged his shoulders. "You're the one who can't stand it. It's something."

"I know some Beatles tunes."

"Beats nothing."

"How about this one? All you need is love, dup, dedup, dedup; All you need is love, dup, dedup, dedup; All you need is love, love; Love is all you need." Beth kept repeating. Soon Ida joined in, and then Troy slapped the side of the Zodiac to the beat, dup, dedup, dedup, and joined in too.

They sang it forty or fifty times as loud as they could. "Okay, that's enough," Troy said. "I can't stand it any more."

The fog was heavy, wet, and quiet. Ida squirmed a little because she had to pee. She felt under the seat for an empty water bottle. "Troy, please turn around. I have to pee." Troy shrugged and turned his back. Beth steadied her as she squatted and peed into the water bottle. Just then she heard the whoosh—a surfacing whale—and then the blow of two more. She fixed her clothes quickly as Troy pointed. "Orcas abeam—fifteen meters out." The whales circled the boat, and then one bumped the side, turning the boat toward the north. Troy held onto a cleat and laughed. "It's Nimpkish, ole Uncle thirty-three. I'll bet Echo is nearby." Another whale bumped the boat again, gently, staring into Ida's eyes with his right eye—a male, smaller than Mike. "That's Echo," Troy said. "Simoom's around here somewhere."

Ida took a deep breath, let it out slowly, and tried to quiet her pounding heart by crossing her arms over her breasts. Something rippled inside her, making her ears ring. The whale bumped again and pushed the boat a couple of meters with the water washing over his back. His eye remained locked on Ida's. A warm, full impression filled her mind. She turned to Troy. "Start the engine. Steer the way he's pushing—they're going to take us somewhere."

Troy fired up the outboard, and sputtering, it pushed them along slowly behind Nimpkish and Echo. They moved silently through the fog for about two hours. Troy shook his head as they ran out of gas and the motor chugged and stopped. Nimpkish and Eco came alongside, one on the starboard and one on the port, moving slowly, and carried the boat along until Troy shouted, "Hey, land ahead. Get the paddles. Hey, look, there's Simoom. Told you she was nearby." Simoom came up behind, pushing gently.

Troy and Beth paddled, the whales turned away, and within ten minutes the boat brushed up against a pebbly shore. Troy jumped out and dragged them up on land and then fell on his back, taking deep breaths, laughing. "Sonofabitch—that was a close one."

"They saved us," Ida said. Beth grinned and nodded her head. Troy stood up and hugged them both and then snapped on the radio. "I'll see if

I raise anyone." Within a few minutes, a familiar voice came back. "Troy, is that you? This is Hazel aboard *Spyhopper*. Where are you?"

"I don't know, but we're lost, but we must be close. This place looks familiar. I'll check around and call you back." Troy disappeared into the fog, returned in about thirty minutes, and grabbed the radio. "*Spyhopper*, I could see Mount Waddington. We're on the other side of Parson Island."

"This is Hazel. Everyone okay?"

"We're fine."

"Joel and I'll jump on the other Zodiac and be there in an hour or so. Hold tight."

They towed the small Zodiac back around Parson Island in the fog, and pulled up beside the lights on *Spyhopper*. The platform was down, and Joel helped Beth. She stepped up as he pushed from behind, his open hand lingering a little too long on her firm, wet bottom. Joel climbed up, and extended a hand to Ida.

"The whales saved us—Nimpkish, Echo, and Simoom," Ida said, beaming. "One pushed and the other two carried us along." Joel looked at Troy. Ida scowled at Joel. "Troy told me the truth—we have the same mother, and you lied to me."

Joel shrugged, taking both of her hands. "Orcas saved you?"

Troy nodded, waving his hands. "She's right, they did. We were on our way to doomsday in Queen Charlotte Sound. I've never seen anything like it. They came soon after we sang a Beatles tune."

"Do you think they heard us?"

"I don't know," Joel said. "Might be synchronous."

Ida turned to Hazel. "I let Echo stare into my eyes. He told me to let him lead us. There was ringing in my ears. It was cold, but his stare warmed me up."

Hazel smiled, putting her open palm over her heart.

Troy rolled a joint, Hazel tied up the boat; Jean smiled, crossed her arms, and then scowled as Joel cradled Ida leaning back into his arms. "I'm so relieved. I thought we were going to die. Now I'm just confused. There's too much. I can't take it all in."

"Let's get you some dinner. We'll see how things look in the morning."

16

oel awakened slowly as he heard someone pad up the stairwell to the pilothouse. The fog had lifted, and through the windshield he could see a few stars in the clouds. He kept his eyes closed and breathed quietly, imagining Beth's soft body leaning back against him as he felt someone sit on the edge of the bed. A hand reached under his blanket and caressed his loins as her face nuzzled into the nape of his neck. "This is our time," Jean whispered.

Joel opened his eyes, smelling her musty hair.

She kept rubbing. "Got anything on your mind?"

Joel didn't move. "How about our usual, unless there's something special on the menu."

"Relax and we'll see."

Jean slipped under the covers. She was naked, warm against his side, and her hand was gentle and firm. She climbed over him and settled, moving back and forth to ease him in, and then buried her face next to his cheek, her hips moving with little awkward jerks. Sometimes he wished she would smooth things out, take a little longer, fuss over him, but even as those thoughts crossed his mind, he was seized by urgent stimulation of the moment, which, of course, always won out. Jean moved faster and faster, whispering in his ear, kissing his neck. "This is it Joel, this is our magic."

Joel looked at the stars and the green light on the radio. The compass light glowed, showing 200 degrees southwest. They had drifted on the anchor. For some reason, Jean felt scratchy, bony, and her thrusts produced little slurping sounds. His face flushed as he began to soften, his relaxation bringing even faster movement from Jean as she cried out, "Joel, Joel—this is it." She flopped full length on his body, wrapped her arms around his neck, and kept on rocking.

Joel shrugged and rolled his shoulders. Her fingernails felt like a lobster pinching his back, but her warmth against him was captivating. She moved a little to the side and reached down with one hand. "Darling, are you all right? That was magnificent."

Joel turned to his side. "I'm sorry, I guess I'm not myself tonight."

"You're just tired. Rest for a while." She stroked him again.

He pushed her hand away. "I love you, Jean, but sometimes I get mixed up. There's a big gap in there between research scientists and lovers. Do you ever get mixed up?"

"I wish we could let people know. If we came out, you know, got married, then I'd be Dr. /Mrs. Joel Martin, and no one would be confused, especially you."

"I thought you would want to keep your own name, or at least hyphenate it."

"I guess that would be suitable. Dr. Jean Jeffry-Martin. Sounds more professional, don't you think?"

Joel sat up, rubbing his chest, and then moved to his captain's chair. "I think I hear someone moving around in the galley."

"It's probably Troy. He knows our every move."

They sat still until the galley was quiet. Then Jean stood up, leaned down, and kissed Joel tenderly, wrapped herself in a blanket, paused as Joel squeezed her bottom, and then clumped down the stairs. "Next time I'll bring the dessert menu," she whispered.

Jean smiled and hummed as she served breakfast—oatmeal with raisins and cinnamon, sliced apples, and cinnamon toast. Joel sat next to Beth. Ida and Hazel sat across, Ida with a green jersey T-shirt, and Hazel with her leg touching Troy's.

"Great news," Troy said. "We've got to get ready for our trip to Robson Bight. Word came on the radio that our permit was granted an hour ago."

The two-week camp at Robson Bight, the protected marine habitat for Orcas, was the highlight of the research effort for Joel and the *Spyhopper* crew. Dozens of killer whales, the northern residents, spent hours at Robson Bight, rolling and rubbing in the shallow water and pebbly beach. It was a perfect place to drop hydrophones and listen to their chirps, squeaks, and songs. Of all places to hear a new dialect, this would be it. Joel was one of the few research scientists granted a permit to camp in the woods near the shore and listen to the whales chirp and play. For Joel and his crew, this was a chance of a lifetime.

"I have to go," Ida said. "I need a ride to Alert Bay so I can get a sea-plane to Victoria."

Beth tipped her head. "You just found out about Troy—why leave now?"

"I want to tell Danny, and I want to find Fred. I need to meet him, to finish the story. I'll come back in a week, if that's all right?" She looked coyly at Joel and Troy.

"The weather's cleared. We'll run you over after lunch. I think there's a flight to Victoria about two o'clock," Joel said.

Troy stood up behind Ida. "Don't get your hopes up. I'm not sure Fred's in Albuquerque."

"I've got to try. I want to meet Mom's old flame, your father. I'll always wonder if I don't try."

17

da turned on her cell phone and called Danny. He answered on the third ring.

"Ida, it's great to hear from you. Where are you?"

"I'm in Alert Bay, and I'm getting on a seaplane to Victoria. I found him, Danny, I found him. It's not Joel Martin, it's a man named Troy Campbell. He used Joel Martin's name at the funeral. He's a friend of Joel's. They knew each other at the same orphanage. Mom sent money every month. He called it guilt money."

"Slow down. I can't keep up."

"I'll tell you all about it tomorrow. I'm coming to Albuquerque. We've got to find Fred."

"Find Fred? He's in Albuquerque?"

"Can you pick me up at the airport?"

"Sure. Just tell me know when. I've missed you so much."

"I'll call you from Seattle when I know my flight time."

"Great news. You found him. I knew you could do it."

"Bye. The plane's here."

Ida ran through the door into Danny's arms. He grabbed her up, hugged her, and twirled her around. They smiled and kissed.

"Let me take your bags," he said.

She slid into the front seat, Danny put her bags in back, and both ER and Jedi squirmed up into her lap and then licked her face. "Hi, little guys. How've you been?" They licked her hands and settled into her lap, both squirming. Ida grinned.

"They're really glad to see you, almost as glad as I am. A month is too long, way too long. Tell me all about your adventures."

Ida talked nonstop all the way to the house, and even into the kitchen as Danny heated up the dinner he had made—pasta, chicken, and mixed vegetables. They sat down, and Ida told him about Beth, the funny couple Dorothy and Paul, driving the yacht, and her new sense of wonder about her interspecies communication with killer whales, especially Mike and northern residents who had saved them from being lost in the fog in Queen Charlotte Sound. "I was afraid we were going to die. That's when Troy told me Mom was his mother. I think he was afraid too, and he thought I should know. Joel knew about Mom from the church charity."

"This is incredible. What are you going to do? Do Jeff and Junior—and your dad—know anything about Troy?"

"No, but Troy watched us walk out of the funeral service. I still can't believe it. He really hated her. Said he was a stain on the family, not good enough to keep. Now I need to find Fred."

"Any idea how?"

"Troy thought his full name is Federico Abeyta, but he goes by Fred, and the last Troy heard, Fred was in an assisted living place somewhere here in Albuquerque. It shouldn't take me long to find out where, if he's here."

"Sounds like a good plan for tomorrow," Danny said. "But I have some other ideas for tonight. Come on, let's brush our teeth. It's getting late." Danny stood up.

"It's only eight o'clock, silly."

Danny opened his arms and Ida melted against his chest. They rocked back and forth. "I've got plans—they'll take a couple of hours. Let's start with the hot tub. It's ready to go."

Ida took off her clothes and snuggled into a fluffy terrycloth robe. Danny stripped and wrapped a towel around his waist.

Ida smiled and did a little sashay with her hips and walked toward him. Danny took one of her hands, pulling her to him and her arm up to his face, and he buried his nose in the crook of her arm, breathing the warm smell of amber and spice, and then kissed her neck through the jasmine scent on the skin under her ear. It had been so long. His anxiety had ramped up some, and he felt a little scattered without her smell nearby. He opened her robe, leaned down, and nuzzled his face under her breasts—jasmine and sage—a scent that traveled directly to the olfactory base of his mind and settled his anxiety better than any drug he had ever taken. They stepped outdoors and slid into the hot tub, the moon making streaks of shadowy light in the rising steam. Ida touched him there, laughing softly. "Seems like you missed me, huh?"

Danny scooted forward. "Miss you?" He grinned. "I feel the most alive when I'm with you."

They relaxed for a while, letting the hot water loosen the knots of the past weeks, the muscles in their backs and shoulders that had carried the weight of not knowing what was next. Ida stood up, her dripping skin sparkling in the moonlight. Danny held her robe as she slipped it on, and they moved to the bed. "Clean sheets. Wow, you thought of everything." They moved quickly through their absence from each other, and Ida dug her heels into Danny's back as he wrapped his arms around her, covering as much of her as he could with his chest and stomach, rocking, clenching his teeth, burying his face in her hair and neck, inhaling the warm, spicy smell of amber on her neck, shaking as she sucked on his earlobe and moaned. Catching his breath, Danny pushed up, taking his weight off her. He took another deep breath—the warm, earthy smell wafting up between their bodies, a jasmine and wood and spice blend he called the essence of Ida. It would last all night and through the next day. Danny looked full into Ida's silver-green eyes, her pupils dilated and quivering. He smiled. "We could make a fortune if we could bottle your smell—works better than any benzos I've ever taken."

Ida's brow furrowed. "I think it's the jasmine smell that does it—has a calming effect. Can't figure out why I smell like that."

Danny slid down and put his head lightly on her stomach, breathing deeply. "Works for me."

Ida arranged herself with his arm around her shoulder and her face on Danny's chest and her hand on his stomach. "You smell pretty good yourself, you know."

The next morning, Danny quietly called Jedi. "Come on, little buddy, we've got hospital visits." Ida was still sleeping, a crumpled sheet over her bare back, and her head buried in a pillow. Her bottom peeked out from the side of the sheet. Danny grinned, crept over to the bed, and kissed Ida's hair and neck. "Hmmm," she said, turning over, her breasts jiggling and then lying to the side. She pulled the sheet over her. "Are you on the way out?"

Danny took a deep breath, the smell of Ida wafting up as she moved the sheet. He hadn't slept so well since she had left.

"Jedi and I have a couple of dog therapy appointments at Presbyterian. I'll call you about noon. Go back to sleep."

Ida pulled a pillow over her face as Danny left the house. She hadn't realized how much tension she was carrying as her body relaxed into the pillow top with new warmth and comfort. She belonged in this bed. She slept another hour, started a fresh pot of coffee, and fixed herself a breakfast of poached eggs on whole-wheat toast. How would she find Fred? She began calling friends who were nurses in hospitals and in nursing homes, and then calling their friends. Her list numbered over thirty, and on call twenty-seven, she got a lead.

"I know I'm not supposed to get into privacy issues, Ida, but I remember a man named Federico at one of those assisted living homes—a beehive on San Joaquin Avenue, over by Animal Humane. I was covering for a friend, and delivered a prescription to the front desk for him."

"Do you remember his last name?"

"Started with an A—Aguilar, Abeyta, something like that."

"Did you meet him?"

"Yes, he came out of his room and introduced himself. He was a delightful man. Very polite and proper. I remember he wore a dark blue robe, and he buttoned the top button on his pajamas."

"That's got to be him. Thank you, Jenny. You're a great help."

"Why are you looking for him?"

"I think he was my mother's boyfriend years ago, and I'd like to meet him."

"I think it is okay to go by there any time. There are only five or six residents."

Ida called Danny. "Are you guys on the way home?"

"Yes, we're almost there."

"Good. I think I found Fred. I want to check it out. I'll call Jeff and tell him we'll come by later. He needs to know everything."

Ida met Danny in the driveway and got in the car. "We need to go over by Animal Humane. I found out there's a beehive home on San Joaquin, and he's probably there."

"That was quick. How did you find him?"

"I just called around and one call led to another. A nurse who is a friend of a friend remembers a man named Federico, and his last name is probably Abeyta."

Danny drove slowly down San Joaquin. A woman was sitting on a porch with two elderly men, and they were playing dominos. "That's probably it. Let's go see."

Ida jumped out, and Danny followed with Jedi. The woman stood up. "Hello, I'm Ida Corley, a registered nurse, and this is Danny. We were hoping to visit Federico Abeyta. I understand he lives here."

"I'm Francis, the daytime attendant. Are you family?"

"In a way." Ida laughed. "He may be my half brother's father. I'm really not sure."

Francis tipped her head, smiling at Jedi. He wagged his tail, looking up at her. "Is he a therapy dog?"

"Certified and everything. We spent the morning over at Presbyterian. It's fine for him to meet your residents." Both men smiled and petted Jedi.

"Come on in. Let me find Fred. You can sit here at the dining room table."

In a moment, Francis ushered out a tall man with white hair and gray eyes. He had a broad grin on his face, and wore blue, ironed pajamas, leather open-toed slippers, and white socks. "Fred, you have some visitors. Sit down here."

"Hello. I'm Fred Abeyta. Whom do I have the pleasure of meeting?"

"I'm Ida—Ida Corley." She watched for a reaction. "My last name is Corley."

Fred grinned and looked up at Francis, as if to ask for help. "Sometimes Fred has a hard time recognizing people."

Ida leaned over. "This is Danny Sandoval. We're getting married in August."

Fred smiled and shook hands with Danny. "Very pleased to meet you. May I pet your dog?"

"Of course. He'll sit up in your lap if you'd like."

Fred sat down. "I'd like that."

Danny put Jedi in Fred's lap, and Jedi licked Fred's hand. "His name is Jedi, like the character from *Star Wars*."

"Jedi, that's a cute name." He looked up. "You said your name is Ada?"

"No, it's Ida, Ida Corley. Do you remember the name Corley? Janice Corley?"

Fred squeezed his eyes shut and then opened them slowly. "That name rings a bell, but I can't place her."

Ida dug in her wallet and brought out a photo of Mom taken a couple of years before she died. "This is the only picture I have with me."

"May I?"

Ida handed Fred the picture. He studied it, licking his lips slowly. "Her eyes look familiar. She has a beautiful smile."

"Do you remember long ago, when you were in high school? I think Janice was your girlfriend."

Fred looked up at the ceiling and wrinkled his nose. He looked at Francis, Danny, and then Ida, and tears began streaming down his cheeks. He looked up again at the ceiling. "Janice, oh, Janice. How I loved you."

Ida put her hand on his arm. "It's okay."

"She's dead, isn't she?"

"Yes, she died almost two years ago."

Fred's eyes dimmed, and then he grinned from ear to ear. "It's a beautiful day, don't you think? This is a nice dog." He petted Jedi. "Such a nice dog. What is his name?"

Francis looked at Ida. "I think that's probably it. His Alzheimer's is quite advanced. I'm surprised he remembered her."

Ida put her hand on Fred. "Tell me, did you ever have any children?"

Fred raised his eyebrows and stroked his chin, still grinning. "Children are so cute."

"Yes, I know, but have you ever been a father?"

Fred fingered the button on his pajama top. "My father worked on the railroad."

Ida turned to Danny. "It's no use. He's almost a blank slate." She stood up, the corners of her mouth turned down and a heavy sadness blurring her eyes.

"That's the most I've seen for months," Francis said.

"Has anyone else ever visited him?" Ida asked.

"Only his lawyer. He handles everything. I think Fred must have put some money away." "How long has he been here?"

"Just over a year. He's gone downhill quickly."

Ida stood up, shook her head, and reached out for Danny's hand. "I guess we'd better go."

"Come back anytime."

They got into the car, Jedi sat on Ida's lap, and they started home. Ida pushed her head back on the headrest and looked into the make-up mirror on the visor. She blinked and started laughing, tears streaming down her cheeks. Jedi licked her face and Danny put his hand on her knee. "What is so funny?"

"It's all so absurd—after thousands of miles I find my half brother—then I find Mom's lover Fred right here in Albuquerque, and he's lost in his own world. I didn't want it to end this way. It's like a huge joke, a joke on me."

"I guess it is kind of funny. What do you want to do?"

"Since the end of this search is a sweet-natured man with no memory, I guess the only thing to do is to accept it. Pure and simple, this is how things are."

"What about Pop?"

"I do have a responsibility to him. Since I stirred this whole thing up, I need to talk with Jeff. Let's swing by his office. I left him a message this morning."

Jeff was cleaning up a mess in his dental lab when Ida and Danny knocked at the door. "Come in and I'll put on some coffee. So you found him?"

"Sure did. His name is Troy Campbell, and he was raised in an orphanage in Victoria. Mom and the church supported them for a long time."

"What's the deal with the guy Joel who came to Mom's funeral?"

"That was Troy. He used Joel's name. Joel was at the same orphanage and helped raise him. They've been friends ever since."

"Are you sure he's Mom's, ah, son?"

"He has letters from Mom to the orphanage."

"What's he like?"

Ida walked over to the wall and studied Mom's picture with her new teeth. "Quiet, withdrawn, intelligent, and has a good heart. He's a walking encyclopedia. Knows everything about the natural surroundings up there—he lives on a research boat called *Spyhopper*, up by Alert Bay. I'll tell you more later. I found Troy's father—Mom's lover, Fred."

"Here in Albuquerque?"

"He's in a group home for Alzheimer patients out by Kirtland. I talked with him, and his memory is blank. He lit up for a minute when I showed him a picture of Mom, but then he faded away."

Jeff began pacing. He fussed with the coffeemaker and started a new pot. "So, what do you think? How do we keep this from Pop?"

"You need to talk with Junior. Troy's happy where he is. He's not looking for any involvement here—he hates Mom, glad she's dead. It's sad. He thinks he was a throwaway, a stain on the family. You and Junior could go meet him someday. I'm going to stay in touch. His girlfriend Hazel has become a good friend, and so has Beth, my traveling companion. She's a social worker. I'm going to make regular visits up there."

"So I guess we can go on like we always have. There's no danger Fred will show up, and, like you say, we could visit up there. There would be no reason for Pop to even wonder."

"Can we count on Junior to keep a secret from Pop?"

"He knows how much this would hurt Pop. He won't say anything."

"I'm going back up to Alert Bay. You're going to think I'm crazy, but I'm fascinated with killer whales. Joel's research is fascinating. He's trying to find a sound, some particular sound that is known to all the killer whales. They all have their dialects, but he's looking for the one chirp or squeak that they all recognize."

Danny stood up and poured some coffee. "That whale Mike—I guess you're convinced you talked with him, huh?"

She looked at Jeff and then Danny. "I'm sure of it. It's mysterious, but I know we were able to touch our feelings and he sent me messages. I've got to find out more."

"From Mike?"

"More than him. Someday I'll tell you guys about it. I can tell you this, though, mental telepathy exists, and it carries across species. The whales understand; they saved our lives."

Jeff looked at Danny. "I believe she's serious. You'll be back for the wedding?"

Ida put her arm around Danny's waist and smiled. "I'll be here. I don't want to miss it."

18

oel moored *Spyhopper* at the dock in Telegraph Cove, south of Alert Bay. They needed to take on fuel and water, do laundry, and gather all the supplies and take them to the Robson Bight camping spot, another 20 kilometers south. Joel and Jean had together secured a two-week research permit, one week each, and this opportunity was the highlight of the summer. With any luck, their hydrophones would capture hours of vocalizations from the A1 Pond - A-12 Matriline, the pod of Scimitar, Nimpkish, Simoom, and her offspring, the same whales that led Troy, Ida, and Beth to safety through the fog. The pod frequented the pebble sea bottom that rose into the Robson Bight Ecological Reserve, and normally appeared during this time, the middle of July. They might even assemble some underwater photos from the new camera setup funded by Joel's UBC grant.

Jean and Hazel drove the borrowed pickup from Telegraph to the end of the forest trail, and there they piled tents, tarps, and equipment onto two carts Joel and Troy had fashioned from old bicycle parts. They followed footpath through the woods to a camping spot in the spruce and the hemlock trees. The site was about 50 meters from the water and adjacent to a clearing bordered on the south by the Tsitika River. After two trips, and setting up two tents, Hazel planted her feet and put her hands on her hips. "I'll gather rocks for a campfire here, and tie a couple of blue tarps on those branches so we'll have a dry place."

"Sounds good," Jean said. "Do you want help unpacking the cooking stuff?"

"No, that's fine. You go on back to the boat. I'll set things up here, and you can come back with Joel in the big Zodiac. Troy's bringing the other Zodiac and the research supplies tomorrow. I'll be fine."

"Sure you're okay here by yourself?" Jean asked.

"I'll be fine. Honestly, I don't mind some quiet time."

Hazel busied herself with cooking supplies, sleeping bags, blankets, lanterns, fuel, and first aid kits. She tied blue tarps at an angle, pulled up dead logs for seating, and dug a couple of shallow latrines deep in the trees. Two ravens flew from tree to tree, cackling and watching her. "You guys behave yourselves."

The next day aboard *Spyhopper*, after lunch, Troy packed equipment in dry bags and placed them carefully in the 14-foot Zodiac. He filled the portable fuel tanks, checked the outboard and steering, and stuffed some protein bars and candy bars into his backpack. "About ready to go?" Joel asked.

"Yup. It's only about twenty kilometers. I should be there by early evening."

"Keep your radio on. I'll bring Jean and Ida in the other Zodiac later tomorrow. Beth is going to stay aboard *Spyhopper*." He grinned at Troy. "This is it. With any luck we'll have hours of recordings by the end of the week. The A-twelve Matriline is nearby. Scimitar, Simoom, and Misty went through Blackney Pass yesterday, so the rest of the pod won't be far behind."

"They love the pebble beach. I'll have stuff set up."

Ida walked up to Troy and tossed her backpack into the Zodiac. "I'm going to ride up with you, okay?" Ida stared at Troy, and he dropped his eyes. "I wasn't planning on company."

"It's better to travel with two people, don't you think? I can carry the handheld radio while you drive."

Troy looked up at Joel, and then back to Ida. "I've single-handed this Zodiac for years." She smiled and stepped quickly into the boat. Joel raised his arms, palms up. "Hey, what can it hurt?"

Troy bit his lip, untied the Zodiac, and hopped in. Ida sat in front, buckled her life jacket, put the radio strap around her neck, and pulled down the brim of her rain hat. It was cloudy and cool.

Troy started the engine, pulled away, and then throttled back to a steady and comfortable six knots, though they were pushing against an ebb tide. It would turn about four pm and be in their favor. He hung his binoculars around his neck and then scanned the horizon as they moved out into Johnstone Strait, staying about 500 meters from shore. "Check the radio, please."

"Radio check, radio check, radio check. This is *Zodiac Two*."

The speaker crackled. "Loud and clear," Joel said. "I've got you loud and clear."

"Roger that. We're about five-hundred meters out heading southeast. Overcast, but not raining. *Zodiac Two* out."

"Travel safe. *Spyhopper* out."

Troy nodded his head, again raising his binoculars. They continued in silence for about an hour. Ida pointed over his left shoulder. "Orcas in the distance."

Troy turned around, focusing his binoculars. "Looks like Scimitar and her pod. I make out six or seven. They seem to be resting."

The sky grayed as the clouds became darker and it started to sprinkle. Ida buttoned up her jacket. "Looks like we're in for some weather."

"Not too bad. It's still fourteen degrees or so."

Ida still hadn't gotten used to centigrade...about 58 F, she thought.

They traveled another hour in silence, Ida staring at Troy, studying his wide forehead, his sloped-up nose, square jaw, and the shape of his head. He had tied his brown and gray hair in a ponytail, now dripping water and hanging out under his black rain hat. He reminded her of Mom.

Soon after four pm, the tide turned, and they began to pick up speed. Troy slowed the outboard. As the Zodiac skipped along with the current, it was quiet and smooth in the little splashes. Ida watched the shoreline pass by, and then on her right, about 400 meters out, seven Orcas swept along, diving and surfacing, fishing for salmon. She could see their misty blows, but they were too far away to hear. Ida pointed, and Troy nodded. "It's them, the A twelves. I can see Nimpkish, Simoom, and Echo. If we were closer, I could tell you the others." Troy raised his face and took a breath, turning the Zodiac closer to shore. "I think the wind's picking up. We're going closer to shore."

After another half hour, the current moved them along at a rapid clip, and soon they were within one km of Robson Bight and 80 meters out. Troy cut the motor. He pointed. "Check it out." Ida looked to her right. Seven Orcas were in a horizontal row facing southeast, agitated and splashing.

About 100 meters further down Johnstone Strait, she saw three other Orcas lined up the same way, facing the seven. Troy stood up. "Wow, here come some southern residents. They're lining up to meet. I've only seen this once before."

Ida turned, looking over her shoulder. "I think it's Mike—look at the huge dorsal fin—and his mom Slick and his little sister Alki. They live by Victoria. How did they get all the way up here?"

Troy pulled out his camera and began snapping photos. "They probably came up through Seymour Narrows or maybe Surge Narrows and the Okisollo channel—who knows why."

Soon the Orcas swam toward each other and began splashing around like children playing in a swimming pool. Ida could hear their squeaks, squawks, and cries in the distance. After a while, they all disappeared, and Ida saw their blows back up the Strait to the northwest. The Zodiac rocked as Troy sat down and put his camera away. He looked up, face glowing, his gray-green eyes sparkling with excitement.

Ida leaned toward him. "This is awkward, but how do we get to know each other? All I know is that you were raised in an orphanage and Joel is your friend."

"There's more you need to know. We'll get to it." Movement on the shore caught their attention. He pointed to the shore where Hazel was jumping up and down, waving her arms, then cupping her hands, shouting.

Troy's eyebrows raised and his face turned white and his jaw dropped. "Oh, shit, hang on!"

Ida turned and saw a wall of water—a huge rogue wave. Within a second, the bow of the Zodiac climbed 12 feet in the air, flipped, and turned end-for-end, spilling everything in the wake of the wave. Ida felt the shock of the icy cold water, convulsed, and opened her eyes to stinging gray salt water and darkness below. She panicked and started thrashing and then felt her life jacket inflate and force her face and shoulders to the surface. She gasped for air, shivering and kicking, her body colder than she'd ever known. Then she remembered. Pull yourself up into a little ball. Keep your core temperature warm. You've got about 20 minutes in this 55-degree water. She tried to relax and hold her knees, but her body shivered and shook. She looked toward the shore, swallowing water from the waves.

Hazel was frantically motioning her in. Maybe she was close enough to swim. Ida reached out and started paddling and kicking. The current carried her slowly down the shoreline. She looked back and saw Troy's life jacket bobbing on the surface, but there was no sign of Troy. The Zodiac was upside down, headed down the Strait. Hazel motioned and shouted. "Come on, Ida, keep moving." Ida swam for her life, but her hands and arms turned numb, and her eyes became blurry. She stopped to take a breath and felt a gentle force at the back of her thighs, something pushing her toward the shore—she picked up speed, holding her head up out of the water—finally a quick push and she let her feet down and touched the bottom. Hazel threw a rope around her, pulling her in to the rocky shore, hugging her, holding her from falling. Ida turned and saw Mike's saddle and dorsal fin. In her mind, a loud thought called out, *You're safe now.* She started weeping, speechless, and then looked to her right. In a swirling, watery valley formed by two whales swimming together, they saw Troy, motionless, eyes closed, head back, swaying in the waves formed by the force of their pectoral fins. It was Slick and Alki. They were bringing him in—seemingly a lifeless body. Hazel and Ida raised their heads as they watched Troy tossed gently toward the shore, half in the water, and then with fluke waves, they swam away. Another thought filled and jarred her mind: *Hurry, he needs help.*

Though soaked, cold, and shivering, Ida helped Hazel drag and carry Troy up the shore and into one of the tents. They were both crying and shaking, using every ounce of strength. "He's barely breathing," she said. "Oh, God, look at his head." Bright red blood covered Troy's face. It was in his eyes and his mouth. A four-inch flap of his forehead and scalp hung loosely, a sharp cut, probably from the prop on the outboard motor. Hazel grabbed the first aid kit and put a handful of 4 x 4's on the wound.

Hazel stood up and took a breath, shaking, teeth chattering, tears streaming down her cheeks. "Okay, Ida, first things first. Get out of those clothes." Hazel dug in a bag, pulled out a few towels, sweatpants, hooded sweatshirts, and wool socks. She helped Ida dry her shivering skin and put on warm clothes. Hazel looked in her eyes with a flashlight. Ida's teeth continued to chatter while Hazel draped a blanket over her shoulders. "Okay, now help me with Troy. He's breathing, but he's hypothermic, so we don't have much time."

They pulled off his wet clothes, laid him on a sleeping bag inside the tent, and covered him with blankets. "Can you work on his head?" Hazel asked. She handed Ida the first aid kit and poured some water into a saucepan. Ida made compresses from hand towels and washed the wound. Troy moved his head. "There's lidocaine in the bag, and syringes." Ida drew up 10 ml of lidocaine and injected it repeatedly along Troy's torn scalp, numbing the skin. Then she found small scissors and cut his hair away. After a few minutes with cold compresses, she started suturing. Hazel lit the Coleman lantern and hung it by a wire close to Troy's head. As the lantern hissed and flickered, Ida carefully cross-stitched his wound with nylon thread, pulling the skin together and using gauze to soak up blood.

Hazel put her ear to Troy's nose and counted his breaths. She felt his weak, slow pulse. She opened one of his eyes and shined the flashlight. "He's in bad shape." As Ida stitched, she glanced up as Hazel took off her jacket, shirt, and gray jersey sports bra. Then she stood up and stepped out of her cargo pants, her gray tights, and her green panties. She reached into a tear-shaped leather bag, took out a small bottle, and daubed fragrant oil onto each brown, oblong nipple, rubbed oil in a circle around her naval, smeared some onto each of her hipbones, and oiled her thighs until they glistened. A heavy sage fragrance filled the tent. She pulled open the blankets and gently lowered herself onto Troy, as though she was letting herself down from a push-up. Her breasts flattened out on his naked chest, covering him, ribs to ribs. Her belly flattened over his, and she arranged her hipbones and thighs to cover his, thigh to thigh. She pulled the blankets over her, rubbed oil under his nostrils, buried her face in his neck with her mouth open, and began to rock ever so gently, chanting an earthy, resonant sound. Ida raised her eyebrows and focused on her stitching. "What is that oil?" she asked.

"It's a helichrysum mixture my grandmother gave me. It's potent, but I've never used it for hypothermia." She moved slightly, burying her face in the nape of his neck on the other side, humming the sound. "Am I in your way?"

"No, I can work around you. Are you breathing on his carotid artery?"

"That's the idea; the sound summons the healing spirits. Everything helps."

The lantern hissed and flickered as Ida stitched and Hazel rocked gently, warming his heart, moving his blood, hoping his nervous system would respond and relax his veins. After a little while, Troy's breathing and pulse became stronger, but he was still unconscious. Hazel raised her face. She was only inches from Ida, and Ida could smell her spicy breath—maybe cloves—and the helichrysum oil that wafted up into the room. Hazel gazed into Ida's eyes and pushed herself up slightly. "I think he's going to make it. He's starting to respond. Are you almost done?"

Ida tied off the last stitch. "That should do it. He's going to have a nasty scar, and we've got to keep this clean." She patted the wound with alcohol patches and then covered it with a cold compress.

"I'm going to roll him to the side. Please hold his head so the wound stays up." Hazel shifted slightly and then reached outside the blanket and into her bag for a bottle of lotion and a towel. She squeezed out a handful, put her hand back under the blanket, and began massaging Troy between his legs. Soon Ida saw the blanket moving up and down, and then Hazel put her other hand under the blanket too. Ida turned her head, face flushing in the shadowy light of the lantern, her mind stretched thin. Here she was, Ida May Corley, having narrowly escaped death, saved by a killer whale who talked to her, holding her unconscious brother's torn scalp with a compress, and watching a marine biology graduate student named Hazel Chartrand, part Kwakiutl, give her half brother a hand job—surreal, not in a million years. She watched out the side of her eye as Hazel rubbed faster and Troy's body arched, shuddered, and then dropped. A quiet moan came from his throat.

"Ancient remedy," Hazel said, smiling. She put her hand on his heart. "His heartbeat's speeding up."

"He can't know I was here for this," Ida said. "Remember, I'm his half sister."

"Don't worry. We'll keep this to ourselves. I won't even tell him." Hazel smiled, stood up, covered Troy with the blankets, dressed, and then took his clothes out and hung them up on the tree branches under the blue plastic tarps. She started a campfire and came back in the tent. Head still in Ida's lap, Troy remained unconscious, but his breathing and pulse had come back to normal. Ida put his head on a pillow, and they straightened up the tent. Hazel took a handheld radio outside and stood nearby in the clearing. "*Spyhopper, Spyhopper, Spyhopper*, this is Campsite One. Do you copy?"

The radio crackled, followed by a muffled voice. "Read you. Have Troy and Ida shown up? Can't raise them on the radio."

"This is Campsite One. They're both here. Repeat, both here. There's a change in plans. Need you to bring the truck. Troy's hurt. Needs medical attention."

"Roger that. Hurt badly?"

"He'll live, but he's got a nasty bump on the head—probably a concussion."

"Roger that. Campsite One, this is *Spyhopper*, on the way."

They pulled up to the emergency door at the Port McNeill hospital. Joel ran inside and returned with two men and a gurney. They lifted Troy off the blankets in the pickup bed, placed him on the gurney, and wheeled him inside. Ida scooted into the driver's seat, moved the truck to the parking lot, and then she and Hazel hurried in. The doctor looked up, frowning, as Ida and Hazel stepped inside the drawn curtain. Troy was on the other side. A nurse asked, "Are you family too?"

"Yes," Ida said. "He is my brother, and she's his fiancée," pointing to Hazel. "I'm a licensed nurse from Albuquerque, New Mexico."

The doctor patted Troy's wound with sterile, wet gauze. "Is this cross-stitching your handiwork?"

Ida nodded her head.

"Nice work. It'll leave a scar, but you closed it up perfectly."

They cleaned up Troy, put him in a gown, and checked his vital signs. The doctor ran his fingers up Troy's legs, felt of his arms, joints, shoulders, and chest. They turned Troy on his side and looked over his back. "All I see is this nasty head wound. I want to get a CT scan. I think he has a concussion, and he'll be unconscious for a while."

The CT scan revealed a hairline fracture of his skull where the prop of the engine hit. His neck was fine, and except for bruises and scrapes from the rocks on the shore, his injuries were limited to his head. The hospital was not very busy, so he ended up in a private room.

"We'll need to keep him for at least a week," the doctor said. "I want to keep him sedated and quiet, and we'll minimize the swelling of his brain as much as possible. I can't say for sure, but it looks like he'll be okay. He must have been moving away from the motor when the prop hit. Lucky, I'd say, eh?"

Joel, Ida, and Hazel sat in the hospital cafeteria for an hour drinking coffee. Hazel turned to Joel. "Everything is set up at the campsite and ready to go. You should go back there with Jean. Two people can handle the hydrophones and recorders. Beth can stay on the radio on *Spyhopper*, and Ida and I'll stay here until Troy wakes up."

"What if he has a brain injury? I should be here."

"Too far for the radio, but I can reach you on your cell phone if you're up on the hill. Let's pick a couple of times."

"I'll be watching him too," Ida said. "You can be back here in a couple of hours if you're needed. You know Troy wouldn't want you to miss any of your time in Robson Bight."

Joel agreed, stopped in Troy's room, and put his hand on Troy's chest. "I know you can hear me. You need to get better soon because I need you. Can't be flaking out on me now. Ida and Hazel will stay with you."

They arranged a couple of chairs in the waiting room and made themselves comfortable. Hazel had brought a backpack with essentials, so she had brushed her teeth, washed her face, and combed her hair back. The light in the waiting room made her black hair shine with a dark purple tint. The skin on her light brown face glowed—flawless. She settled back in a chair and smiled. "Why did you say I was Troy's fiancée?"

"The doctor asked if we were all family, and that just popped into my mind." Ida raised her eyebrows. "Would that be so bad?"

"No, that wouldn't be bad. I just hadn't heard it before. Troy and I get along well, and he talks with me about things. We have a lot in common."

"Like what?"

"He knows everything about the natural world around here. He's like a nature encyclopedia. We love to watch eagles together. We don't talk, just watch. He carries on and chatters with the ravens, the muskrats, and the sea otters. He knows all the trees, the flowers, the grasses, and the geology. He has even told me things about Kwakiutl history. Troy knew that the potlatch was outlawed by the Canadian government in 1884, and the last one was in 1921 in Alert Bay."

"Potlatch—the giving ceremony?"

"It was more than that. Potlatches mourned the dead, celebrated new chiefs, and maintained community and social hierarchy. Troy said the idea of giving more extravagantly than someone else was too competitive for him, but at least giving was higher on the spiritual scale than taking. People acquired blankets, food, canoes, and carved cedar boxes so they could give them to others. The more you gave, the richer you were."

"That's different—get stuff so you can give it away."

"Troy said the Orcas got it right. They stay together in families so they can give each other what they need. The boys stay with their mothers until they die, the girls have babies that stay in the pods, the fast ones herd fish to the slow ones and they all protect the calves while they nurse."

"He's told you all that? Seems to me he doesn't talk much."

"Most of the time. But when we're together, he opens up." Hazel giggled. "Sometimes he lays his head in my lap, looks up into the heavens, and tells me about all kinds of things."

"Has he talked much about our mother?"

"Doesn't say much about her—he's angry, I know that. She wrote letters about you and your brothers. He has pictures from when you were little."

"Pictures?"

"He has an album, about ten pages or so. He keeps the album down in the engine room with his other stuff."

"Have you seen it?"

"One night we got a little stoned, and I was with him down there. He paged through it. Told me these people were his family, but he hated his mother."

"Pictures of my brothers?"

"We laughed at the ones with Jeff and Junior and Goofy at Disneyworld. He said they looked as goofy as Goofy."

"Did you see any pictures of me?"

"There's a page of when you were two or three in a T-shirt, in a sand-box and on the swings—you didn't have any pants on."

"Any others?"

"There's one of you in your cheerleader outfit, high kicking in your short skirt, one when you graduated from high school, and one with your nursing school graduating class."

"Did he think I was goofy too?"

"No, he didn't say you were goofy."

"Did he say anything?"

"He said his sister was jailbait."

"Jailbait? Really?"

"Yeah, sorry, but from your pictures, he could see you were putting it out there."

"All these years. I never realized."

"Troy's a good man. I could be his fiancée. Of course, he'd have to ask me, or maybe I'll have to ask him. We'll see."

"Did you stay with him in the engine room?"

Hazel smiled and blushed through her brown skin. "Up until that night, he seemed reserved, almost distant."

"That night?"

"I was surprised. He was talking, resting his head in my lap, when out of nowhere he reached up, touched my face with more tenderness than I've ever felt, sat up, and kissed me. It was so sweet."

"And then?"

"One thing led to the next. I got up early and slipped into my cabin before light."

Two days and nights passed before Troy woke up. Ida and Hazel wandered around town, went to the library, bought a few new clothes, and spent time in the museum. At 10:30 am on the third day, Troy opened his eyes to Ida's green eyes and Hazel's gentle smile. His arms were restrained, and his eyes darted around the room. He wiggled his hips. "You're in the hospital in Port McNeill," Ida said. "You have a concussion. They restrained you so you wouldn't move, and you have a catheter."

Hazel put her open palm on his chest. "You're going to be okay."

"How long...have I been out?"

"Three days. Remember the huge wave? The prop on the outboard hit your head."

"You won't believe this," Ida said, "but Mike and Slick and Alki saved us—Mike pushed me, and Slick and Alki carried you in—unbelievable." She put her hands on her heart.

Troy raised his eyes, looking at the thick, white bandage on his forehead. Ida touched the bandage with a feather-light finger. "You have a four-inch gash in your scalp. You'll probably have a scar."

"Ida sewed it up," Hazel said. "You've got a hairline crack in your skull. It would have been a lot worse if you weren't so thick-headed."

Troy smiled. "The whales..." His eyelids drooped, and he slept.

The next morning Troy's restraints were gone, his bed was cranked up, and he had a small bowl of chicken soup and a little dish of green Jell-O on a brown tray in front of him. "I was just sitting down to breakfast. Care to join me?"

Both Hazel and Ida beamed.

The doctor came in, shined a bright penlight in Troy's eyes, felt his pulse, and jotted some notes on a clipboard. "How are you feeling?"

He touched his bandage. "I'm feeling a lot better except for this headache."

"I'll give you something for that. As soon as you can walk up and down the hall without wobbling, we'll get you out of here. Plan on another three days."

"Okay, doc." Troy scooped up a spoonful of Jell-O and held it up. "Would you like a bite of my Jell-O?"

The doctor grinned. "No thanks. This hospital food is horrible."

Jailbait. Really? Ida told Hazel and Troy she would be gone for the day—she needed some time to herself. She caught a ride from the hospital to the ferry and bought a ticket for the 10:25 am crossing to Alert Bay. She stood by the window, watching the sunlight streak and dance over the blue-green waves. It was a warm day, and she planned to walk along the shore and take in the scenery.

The ferry crossing was only 45 minutes. She stepped off and headed down the dock to the boardwalk, the wood sidewalk built along the shore with shops and seating areas. She walked to the bright red Alert Bay drug store, bought a root beer, and sat on a wooden bench, purple and yellow flowers hanging from planters and fluttering in the breeze. She pursed her lips as if to whistle, and then relaxed into a gentle smile. There was so much. She had a half brother and he was alive. Whales had drawn her into mysterious places that frightened her at first, but now a source of inscrutable curiosity, whispers of wisdom from the world of spirit. Beth, Joel, and Troy, each in their own way, had climbed the wall in her mind and softened the fear that her life was coming apart. Poor Dorothy. Maybe she and Paul would find some help. And that silly Greg. He just showed up at the right time to make Beth glow with happiness. She was so at ease with herself, standing by that shower, naked and wet, smiling, looking at her with peaceful satisfaction through her moist blue-gray eyes.

Ida finished her root beer and climbed off the boardwalk, down on the rocky shore, walked back toward the ferry dock, and sat down on a gray-white driftwood log. The tide was slack, and she watched tiny bugs skitter and scoot in the little tide pools. Then she saw it, drying in the sun. A few feet back from the water's edge, a small brilliant purple starfish clung to a flat gray rock that was green and white and red with algae and lichen. She kneeled down, touched the starfish, and tried to pull it loose. It clung onto the rock, mightily resisting her pull, strong and stubborn. A wave splashed her shoes, and she looked up to the horizon. In the distance, a pod of killer whales was making its way, probably feeding. Their misty blows looked like puffs of smoke in the sunlight, and their rhythmic movement tugged at her. She pulled at the starfish. Jailbait? Is that how he saw her? Is that who she was, underneath? Could it be that her young teenage body took her mind hostage? She thought of the men she had known, one by one. Did she need them? Could she remember how they felt, how they smelled? No, she could only remember their desire her for her; she had clung onto that desire as they had clung onto her. As she watched Kevin's fascination in the tent, as she watched older men at the church stare at her breasts, as she changed into sexy clothes in the church bathroom, as she kicked high in her skimpy cheerleader skirt, she had created escape routes from her mother's frowning gaze. Why was she still clinging? What was she running from? Maybe her mother's control and judgment. She had to cling to something—the closest thing, her body and what it did to men. That would put her in control, and that, she came to believe, made her free.

She loved Danny dearly. Why didn't he seem like enough? Holding on didn't make her free—it made her miserable, and she was tired. Could she stand tall, naked, beautiful, strong, and natural, like Beth? Ida carefully peeled the starfish tentacles one by one from the rock, and carefully tossed this fragile little creature out into the water. *You have to let go or you'll get cooked in this sun. You don't want to end up as fish bait.*

Ida ate a leisurely lunch at a restaurant in the hotel, walked some more, and took a late afternoon ferry back to Port McNeill. A woman she met on the ferry gave her a ride back to the hospital, and she found Hazel dozing in the waiting room. She didn't disturb her and went into Troy's room. He was playing solitaire with a blue deck of cards on a tray on his lap. He smiled and pointed to a chair. "Good to see you. I just got back from walking up and down the hall. I think I can get out of here tomorrow."

"Great. Joel can take us back to Robson Bight." Ida took a breath and smoothed her hair. "I took a ferry ride to Alert Bay for a little quiet time. Walked around the town and sat on the shore. It was nice. I've been wondering. On the Zodiac, before we got swamped by that wave, you said there was more. You said we'd probably get into it. What did you mean?"

Troy gathered up the cards. "I've been thinking about how to tell you. I've decided I'll just blurt it out."

"Okay, I'm listening."

"Fred is your father."

Ida folded her hands in her lap, took a breath, and turned white as Troy's starched sheet. "Are you sure?"

"I'm sure. Our mother told me, in a letter."

"How did, I mean when did...how did that happen?"

"Mom and Pop had a weeklong fight about something, and Fred caught Mom in a weak moment one night at church. She said they went to his house and he comforted her. That's how she said it. Comforted her. He sure as hell did a lot more than that, and she let him. She found out she was pregnant with you just before she and Pop made up. There, I said it. We have the same mother and father."

Ida dropped her head into her hands.

19

oel parked the truck and made his way down the hill to the campsite near the estuary of the Tsitika River. Though the afternoon was bright, the dense hemlock, fir, and red cedar blocked the sun, making bright spots and shadows on the sword fern. A breeze filled the air with the sharp scent of fir and cedar. They had camped in among hemlock trees, just behind a span of tufted hairgrass, meadow barley, and red fescue. The small open area led to alluvial and gravel deposits that formed the pebble rock beds where the Orca pods loved to rub, frolic, breed, squeal, squawk, and whistle out shrieks. More than 180 Orcas visited this area every summer, a place rich with an array of sounds from different pods.

Jean greeted Joel on the trail. "How's Troy?"

"He has a concussion, and he's still unconscious, but the doctor says he's going to be okay."

"That's a relief," Jean said.

"The scalp wound is pretty bad, but he's stitched up, and there's no infection. I feel guilty leaving him, but he's in good hands with Hazel and Ida, and our time here is limited."

"Sit down and have some soup," Jean said. "I'll bring you up to date."

Joel sat on a log with a cup of beef stew and a stack of soda crackers. "Are the recorders running?"

"I've got four hydrophones in the water, and Troy rigged voice sensors so they only come on if there's a certain decibel level. I've checked the earphones. They're picking up everything."

"We put up branches for screens," Jean said. "If you go down by the water and look back, you can't see the campsite. I hung up blankets by the recorders, so you can't hear a thing. If we stay quiet, we should be able to catch hours of sounds."

"This is great," Joel said. "I'm worn out—need to sleep for a while before I start listening."

"I laid out your sleeping bag in the tent. Want some company for five minutes or so?"

Joel smiled. "I will later." He was asleep as soon as he slipped into his sleeping bag. He awoke about three am, bundled up against the cool night, and sat behind the large tent in a green, canvas director's chair with his earphones on over a blue wool watch cap. He kept his notebook on his lap, noting the time and the sounds so he could follow the recordings later. His mind drifted to the times years ago when he sat quietly listening to Bjossa and staring into her eye. She had led him to believe that the elusive sound—the Holy Grail—actually existed. It was a rare, musical, and resonant sound, she said, in a midrange octave, separated into measures with chirps, and it served to remind the pods and clans that they were spiritually connected to each other, to all living things, through all time, and through all imaginable space in the universe. Bjossa would not have led him astray. She loved him.

Over the next three days, Jean watched over the equipment and made sure Joel was comfortable while he listened.

Unknown to Jean, Joel used 250 micrograms of LSD every eight hours so he could focus across the whole spectrum of reality. Except for the scratching of his pen, for occasional breaks to go to the latrine, and quick pauses to eat something Jean prepared, he was quiet, motionless, and utterly focused on his life's work.

A storm arrived. The wind, rain, and waves all rose up at once, the waves crashing on the shore and the wind flapping and rippling the tents with fury. They spent the rest of the day and night keeping the tents staked down, covering equipment, reading, dozing, heating up soup on a tiny camp stove, and staying warm. Had there been a dry place, Joel would have paced. As it was, he muttered at the wind and wrote things in his notebook. The hydrophones were silent. In the morning, Joel followed one of the wires into the water and discovered the hydrophone was gone. So were the other three. He tramped back to the tent and looked at Jean with his hands on his hips. "Did you bring any more hydrophones?"

"No, I thought four would be more than adequate."

"They're all gone. The waves jerked the wires loose. We've got nothing."

Jean looked up at the cloudy sky and chewed her lips. "There's a white plastic box with four new hydrophones back on the boat, under the tarp in the corner by the bookcase."

Joel took the handheld radio and climbed up the hill, searching for a reasonable line of sight. He called five times, "*Spyhopper, Spyhopper, Spyhopper*, this is Campsite One. Do you read me?"

He heard a crackle and Beth's weak voice. "This is *Spyhopper*. I can hear you."

"Listen carefully. Go over by the bookcase near the galley. Lift up the blue tarp. Look in the white box."

"Hold on, I'm looking."

"There's supposed to be four hydrophones. They're brand-new in boxes. You'll see a picture on the front."

"All four of them are here."

"I'm on my way. I'll see you in four or five hours. Out."

Joel returned to the campsite, frowning, agitated. "I'm taking the truck to Telegraph Cove. I'll borrow a dinghy, go back to *Spyhopper*, and get the hydrophones. I should be back by morning. We can't waste any time."

Joel turned and trudged up the shadowy trail through the tall cedars and fir trees. He jumped in the truck, and bounced up the old logging road, holding onto the steering wheel.

The harbormaster at Telegraph Cove knew Joel, and loaned him a 16-foot aluminum boat with a 35-horsepower Evinrude. "The gas tank is full. See you in a little while."

He pulled up alongside *Spyhopper* within a half-hour. The sun was bright on the quiet water, and the boat was motionless. Beth greeted him with a smile. She wore cut-off jeans, blue tennis shoes, and a white T-shirt with no bra. "You made good time. I've got the box right here."

Joel stood up in the boat and wrestled one end of the platform.

"Could you catch the other end?" Beth helped drop the platform, extended her hand, and helped him aboard.

Joel looked around. "Wow, what happened to *Spyhopper*? She looks like she had a bath."

Beth laughed. "I decided to make myself useful."

The deck was clean, the galley was clean, and everything was shipshape.

Joel looked at Beth, his eyes lingering. She took on a glow in the sunlight, giving the impression she was stronger and wiser than she let on. Maybe it was the waning effects of the LSD, but Joel saw an aura around Beth that shimmered with gold, purple, and a silvery mist that reminded him of the blow of killer whales in a brilliant sunset. Her radiance stunned him. He swallowed and rubbed his mouth with his hand. He could almost taste her warm, salty skin, the tiny little drops of perspiration sparkling above her smiling lips. If he listened carefully, he knew he would hear the low whistle of air in her lungs and the steady hum of her life force.

"Would you like something to eat? I made some egg salad sandwiches."

"Sure, that would be great." He sat down at the table in the galley, and Beth put out a plate of sandwiches in the middle and poured fresh coffee.

"Thank you. This is nice. I could use a few minutes to settle down before I head back."

Joel couldn't take his eyes off of Beth. He chewed his sandwich in a trance, smelling a hint of her lavender.

"Can you make it back by dark?"

Her question startled him. "If I leave in the next hour, I will be fine. I'm wasted. I'm going up to the pilothouse for a quick nap."

Joel stretched out on the seat, took a breath, clasped his hands over his chest, and drifted off, an image of Beth in his mind. In what seemed like only a few seconds, he heard Beth. "It's been forty five minutes. Probably time to go."

Joel looked at the clock, and stood up. "Right, thanks for waking me. I need to get back and hook up these hydrophones." He hurried down the stairs.

Beth helped Joel lower the box into the boat, and Joel covered it with a blue, plastic tarp, and secured the box with a couple of bungee cords. Joel started the motor, smiling and waving at Beth. "See you in a few days."

He parked the boat, carried the box to the truck, and drove back to Robson Bight. He parked the truck, grabbed the box, and made his way down the trail. It wasn't heavy, just awkward. Joel breathed deeply, smelling the red cedar, the Douglas fir, and the blanket of pine needles on the ground. Everything reminded him of Beth. She was his age, remarkably beautiful, and he couldn't get her out of his mind.

Jean greeted him with quick scrutiny. "You look like you're no worse for the wear. We've got two hours until dark if you want to get these hooked up. The fish stew will stay warm by the fire."

Joel put on his wet suit, and they set to work stringing new wires and placing the hydrophones in areas protected by rocks and kelp. They finished as darkness crept down the embankments and into the camp. Everything checked out. Jean served bowls of stew and they turned in early, this time well rested for the "five or ten minutes" that Jean had in store for him. She was a good friend and often knew his needs before he did.

Joel settled into his chair in the gray early dawn. The sky was clear, showing the promise of a good-weather day. He put on his earphones and opened his notebook, starting a new page. He turned as he felt a touch on his shoulder. Jean handed him a steaming mug of coffee with milk and sugar and a large cinnamon roll. He nodded his head and put the paper plate on his lap. When he was sure he was alone, he tore a microdot of LSD from a small piece of paper he kept buttoned in his camp shirt pocket. He listened for ten hours, interrupted only by latrine breaks.

They made their way down the path at noon. Ida and Hazel each held one of Troy's hands as they stepped slowly. As they came within earshot, Troy called out. "Anybody home down there?"

Joel and Jean rushed over and hugged Troy, and then led him over to a chair by the smoldering campfire. "I'm not helpless, you know. The doctor said I'm fine. May be a little dizzy now and then, but that's it."

"Troy is my brother," Ida blurted out. We have the same mother *and* the same father."

Everyone looked around at each other, smiling. "We all knew," Hazel said, "but it was Troy's place to tell you."

Troy grinned, taking her hand. "You might as well get used to it."

Ida swung his hand up in the air, laughing. "Can I see your photo album some day?"

"Sure. But you'll have to come back. Your territory has expanded, Ida. There is part of you here now." Troy turned to Joel. "Okay, what can I do to help?"

"Check over the recorders and make sure they're okay. You can put on some headphone and listen if you'd like. Jean made turkey sandwiches."

Early in the morning Ida awoke with a new eagerness for whatever what next—travel home, hot tub with Danny, wedding, back to work. As she made preparations to leave, Joel saw she was crying as she folded clothes, putting them into her backpack. Jean and Hazel stepped up near her. Joel put his arm around her, and Troy faced her. "We are all going to miss you. I hope you realize what your visit has meant to everyone."

Ida sniffled, wiping her nose. "I'm the lucky one. I have a brother, new friends, and a clear mind. Can you believe I'm sleeping again? My nails are growing out."

Hazel put her hand on her heart, bowing her head slightly. "My heart is filled with you. Thank you for the gifts of friendship and your brother—gifts of a lifetime."

Jean offered both hands, shook Ida's hand, and then hugged her. "Come back anytime," Jean said. "You're always welcome in my galley."

Troy took a couple of steps, and Joel stopped him. "Are you sure you're all right to drive?"

"Yeah, I'm fine."

Ida and Troy started up the trail. "Wait up," Hazel said. "I'll ride along."

They got coffee and a sweet roll as they waited for the seaplane in Port McNeill. Ida had a long day ahead. Port McNeill—Victoria—Seattle—Albuquerque. She stood up. "I'll be back in a minute. I want to call Beth." She answered on the second ring.

"How are you doing all alone out there?"

"Actually, I'm enjoying the time alone. I was worried I'd be frightened, but I'm not. I've come alive again thanks to you."

"Greg might have had something to do with that."

"It's you that brought me into this place, and he helped me walk through the darkness. Greg was a happy coincidence."

"Was?"

"Things are changing, Ida. Spiritual forces are at work."

"Is it Joel?"

Beth laughed softly. "He keeps swimming by, catching my eye. He's ready for something new, something deeper, don't you think?"

"Poor Jean. She's so dedicated to him, and so sweet. Do you think she knows he'll never mate for life, at least with her?"

"Yeah, I think she knows," Beth said. "I'm sorry for her, and her pain, but I'm guessing she'll come to know a new freedom."

Ida looked around and lowered her voice. "I see a gentle love between them, but for Joel it's more like friends with benefits. Their minds don't match. It would be a married life of never-ending frustration."

"It's as though they swim in the same ocean but come from different cultures," Beth said. "She swims with the scientists, and Joel swims with the stars—he should've been a poet."

"Promise you'll send an email. I want to know everything about you and Joel—everything."

"Will do," Beth said, laughing. "There's some good news about the McHughs. I talked with Dorothy in Port Hardy. They've parked *Destiny* for a while in the harbor up there. Paul decided to go into a rehab center. Says he wants to stop drinking."

"Wow, what brought that on?"

"He broke down one night and told Dorothy he wanted to go see the kids. Maybe Christmas. Said he wants to get the family back together."

"Is Dorothy with her sister?"

"She stays there, and takes care of *Destiny*. Her brother-in-law—you know, he's the experienced captain—told Paul he would guide them around the island next summer if everything works out with the rehab."

"Did you tell Dorothy hello from me?"

"Yes. I said we were both praying for them."

"The plane is landing. I've got to go soon."

"Ida, I love you."

"Me too. Send that email."

Ida put her phone in her pocket, turned, and Hazel took Ida's hands. Hazel's face softened, glowing, alluring. "You know we are destined to stay together. The eagles, the whales, all of us aboard *Spyhopper*. We're a new family."

Troy smiled. "Yeah, just call us the Hazel pod, and Hazel's the top female in the matriarchal line. We'll all be traveling with her."

The plane pulled up to the dock. Troy carried her bag, and Hazel held her hand as she stepped aboard. "What's next?" Troy shouted over the engine noise.

"Next? I have to go back to work, and I'm going to get married. I'm bringing my new male Danny into the Hazel pod." She grinned, eyes glowing. "He's good breeding stock."

20

*H*er curls of shiny blond hair sparkled in the sunlight as Ida and Pop walked across the yard. The bright white paper rolled out made a path to where Danny and the preacher stood. Junior and Jeff were both best men, and two of Danny's friends played guitars as 90 guests turned in their seats to watch Ida walk slowly down the aisle to Danny, both of whom were grinning ear to ear. They loomed larger than life, tall, robust, healthy, and seemed to make the sun shine even brighter. A cool breeze brought a clean, crisp odor from the pinon and cedar trees. Purple asters and yellow daisies waved gently near the bright red roses that grew in the soil enriched by Mom's ashes.

Ida's bright green eyes focused on Danny, and as she caught his eyes, she knew that no matter how deep he could see inside her, he would see nothing but a clear mind. The walled-in space had vanished, and the frustrations packed in there had disappeared and were buried in the deep gray water of Johnstone Strait, each one stretched thin and stripped of their power by singing Orcas, raising to the surface like bubbles, bursting, and scattering into the four winds. The killer whales were now anchors for her sense of wonder, and now there was only one man who desired her, and he was enough. Fresh ways of seeing had brought her gently into a bright blue stream of life, making her buoyant, floating in and through shimmers of people, the beat of the music, and the sweet smell of roses. Danny's eyes glistened as she held the muscles of her father's arm as he matched her pace, step by step. Her heartbeat drummed a cadence for her white patent leather shoes, the swish of her white lace dress, the bounce of her rounded, modest cleavage, and the steady breath from her slightly parted lips.

Was she in the gentle breeze or was the breeze in her? Everything softened as she seemed to enter a penumbra, as though all of her edges were dissolving, leaving only shapes moving along on the white paper. She was happy. She was in love with so much more than before, not only Danny, but the life she could see ahead.

They exchanged rings. "You may kiss the bride," she heard as Danny gently pressed his lips to hers. She was married. She had said vows, the preacher had talked, Danny repeated vows, the little dogs ER and Jedi had run to them with their wedding rings tied to their collars, they had put the rings on each other, but the words "You may kiss the bride" were the only words that formed clearly enough to rise up from the gentle fullness around her. She flicked her tongue between Danny's lips in a way no one could see, and then they turned, smiled, and looked into the crowd of clapping and hooting people standing by their beige metal folding chairs.

Ida took a step and stopped abruptly, stunned. On the back row, blocked by the crowd, she saw Troy and Joel jumping above the crowd grinning and waving, as though they were spyhopping. In the aisle ahead, Hazel and Beth were dancing and laughing, slapping high-fives, twisting and turning, and flipping their bottoms at Ida and Danny. On the opposite side, Jeff and Junior were moving Pop inside to the reception tables and the food. As she and Danny began walking again, Ida's mood dropped into impending doom—Pop would find out. The day would be ruined. The wedding would become a dark, painful memory. The magic dropped out of the sunlight like a large stone falling through clear water.

Ida and Danny stood and greeted everyone as they passed along the reception line. Pop, Jeff, and Junior were first, and Troy, Hazel, Joel, and Beth were at the end of the line. Ida took a breath as they walked over to the gift table where Pop was arranging boxes and envelopes. Ida took little breaths, raised her eyebrows, and held tight to Danny's arm, trying to keep her balance. Guitar music had started; people were laughing and filling their plates with food. Ida jumped as Beth came up from behind. "I'm so happy for you."

Ida gulped and her heart sank as Pop waved her over to the gift table where Troy and Joel stood in a crowd a few short steps from Pop. She pulled Danny along as she approached Pop, dropping her face. There was no escaping or coming back from this moment, a moment that could crush Pop's soul with waves of pain. She looked at Jeff through eyes clouded by fear. Ida squeezed Danny's hand, and her face turned ashen as Troy approached the table. Pop's face brightened with a broad smile as he leaned in toward Troy, taking his hand. "So you're Troy. I'm your stepdad, Roy Corley. Been looking forward to this day for forty-four years."

Troy nodded. They smiled at each other, shook hands, and then with all the ease of longtime friends, they laughed, hugged, and slapped each other on the back. Ida froze. She took shallow breaths, puzzled.

Pop turned to Ida "Open your gift," he said. An old blue comforter was wrapped around the cedar chest, the comforter that Mom had knitted years ago—the one Ida had kept on her bed as a child. Ida pulled the comforter away. Clean varnish on the cedar chest reflected the sunlight. The copper straps and hinges were polished and spotless.

"Open it," Pop said.

Lips quivering, Ida opened the top and peeked inside. There was a letter addressed to her in Mom's handwriting. She opened the envelope, hands shaking, eyes darting to Pop's face and then back to the letter.

My dearest Ida,

Pop is the father who raised you and loves you. Fred was only a sperm donor and I was young and foolish. Pop knew everything when you were born. When you find Troy, please ask him to forgive me.